I0651997

Howard Pease

Tales of Northumbria

Howard Pease

Tales of Northumbria

ISBN/EAN: 9783337344795

Printed in Europe, USA, Canada, Australia, Japan

Cover: Foto ©Andreas Hilbeck / pixelio.de

More available books at **www.hansebooks.com**

TALES OF
NORTHUMBRIA

BY

HOWARD PEASE

METHUEN & CO.
36 ESSEX STREET, W.C.
LONDON
1899

TO

EARL GREY

EVER KEENLY INTERESTED IN WHATEVER

CONCERNS HIS NATIVE COUNTY

THESE SKETCHES OF NORTHUMBRIAN CHARACTER

ARE DEDICATED BY THE AUTHOR

CONTENTS

The tales that go to make up this small volume have already appeared in print : the first part of the Introduction, 'A Long Main,' 'In Memoriov'm,' in the *National Observer*: 'The Protégé,' in the *Queen*; 'Quaker John and Yankee Bill,' 'T'Owd Squire,' 'An Ammytoor Detective,' in the *Newcastle Courant*; 'À l'Outrance,' in the *Newcastle Weekly Chronicle*; and the remaining six in the *Newcastle Daily Leader*. I desire to tender my thanks herewith to the various editors concerned.

L.

TALES OF NORTHUMBRIA

NORTHUMBERLAND

I T is generally admitted that your Northumbrian pre-eminently possesses the
quality which the pious but worldly Scotch-
man was used to pray for, namely, 'a guid
conceit o' hissel'.'

It is the more unfortunate, therefore, that
of late years a considerable landslip should
have taken place in the ground whereon his
reputation rested.

The local poet no longer hymns the
'Champions o' Tyneside,' for Chambers and
Renforth and other heroes have long since
departed, leaving 'no issue.'

I

Advancing civilization, again, has, it is to be feared, made havoc of the proud insularity of the Northumbrian squirearchy.   No longer are they content, like the Osbaldistones of yore, to devote themselves to cellar and stable, to stay at home, contemptuous of London and its politics, of travel and of new ideas.   'Markham's Farriery' and the 'Guide to Heraldry' have lost their pristine charm, and the Northumbrian is, as a consequence, foregoing his ancient characteristics merely to become provincial.

'Geordie Pitman' alone makes a stand against all modern innovation.   Firm in his pele tower of ancient superiority, he is still convinced of the superiority of all things Northumbrian.

'Champions' may have died out elsewhere, and patriotism be decayed in the higher social ranks, but in the pit-village there still lingers an admirable quantity of the old self-love.

In each separate village you may find some half-dozen self-styled 'champions' who will match themselves against 'any man in the world' for £10 or £15 a side at their own particular hobby or pastime.

Defeat has little effect upon a 'champion': like Antæus, he picks himself up the stronger for a fall, and having advertised himself in the papers as 'not being satisfied' with his beating, challenges another attempt forthwith.

*　　*　　*　　*　　*

Now this self-satisfaction—though somewhat decayed of late—is probably one of the oldest strains in the Northumbrian character, having been developed, doubtless, in the first instance, under stress of constant raid and foray, and but little affected thereafter—owing to the remoteness of the county both from the universities and from London—by the higher standards of softer and more civilized centres.

After this, the next most predominant trait is a love of sport, for which the climate, together with the physical conformation of the county, may be held responsible; for the open aspect of the plain, the crown of bare western hills, the wind-swept moorland and the sea, suggest a life of hard endurance and fatigue, the strenuous toil of the hunter, the keen excitements of the chase.

Still, as of old, the wide and spreading grasslands try horse and rider with a tempting challenge, as of one who cries, 'Come, who will tire first?' The music of the hounds sweeps down the brae: 'Yoi—yoi—yoi!' quivers the cry from the streaming pack. Onward the rider gallops, the plover perchance rising at his horse's heels, the long note of the curlew sounding in his ears, the breath of the west wind racing in his nostrils ; he may see on this side the purple bar of Cheviot, on the other the blue, flat line of the sea, and therewith—if ever in his life—may taste of the primeval joy of living—of the joy of the early hunter who lived with his horse as with a comrade, drew from the sea the 'sacred fish,' from the moorland the 'winged fowl,' and knew not discontent.

The beauty of the southern counties is not to be met with here.

The south is the well-dowered matron, the north a bare-headed gipsy-lass, freckled with sun and wind, who 'fends' for her living with strategies of hand and head.

Still, in the northern blood, the heritage of the 'raid' and the 'foray' abides, and still, as of old, are the children of the Borderland nursed by the keen wind of the moorland and the sea. 'Hard and heather-bred' ran the ancient North-Tyne slogan; 'hard and heather-bred—yet—yet—yet.'

'SO you're a county family?' I echoed, and, though it may have been impolite, I could not forbear a smile, for never had I seen County Family so well disguised before.

'Ay,' replied Geordie Crozier, 'I is,' and forthwith proceeded to search in the pocket of his pit-knickerbockers for his 'cutty.' He had just come up to 'bank' from the 'fore-shift,' and was leaning on a waggon on the pit-heap, about to have a smoke before going home for a 'wesh,' dinner, and bed. 'The last ov us,' he continued, having lit his pipe, 'that had Crozier Hall was grandfeythor—Jake Crozier, of Crozier Hall, was his name an' address, an'—an'—I's his relics.'

I glanced at the 'relics' afresh—six foot two if he was an inch, and broad in proportion, a magnificent pair of arms—he was champion hewer at the colliery—with legs to match, though slightly bowed through the constant stooping underground. Under the mask of coal-dust his eyes gleamed like pearls, and a thrusting lower lip, backed by a square jaw, gave evidence of determination and the faculty of enjoyment. A short, well-trimmed beard put the finishing touch to 'the Squire,' for so his friends styled him, half in jest.

'Well, and how was it lost?' said I. 'Was "cellar and stable," the good old Northumbrian motto, his epitaph? Or did your grandfather take an even quicker road to the bailiffs?'

'Grandfeythor was like us, I b'lieve; he was a fine spender but an ill saver, an' he had a h—— ov a time till the mortgages gave oot, for he was a tarr'ble tasteful man — lasses, greyhounds, an' horses, racin',

drinkin', cockin', an' card-playin' were aal
hobbies ov his at one time or another, but
what was warse than aal this put togither
was that he never wud be beat. Everything
he had must be the best, an' the fact that
anythin' belonged to him was quite enough
to prove to him it was the best o' the sort i'
the county. Well, for a while as a young
man things went well wi' him. He win the
Plate* two years runnin', an' many was the
cock-fight an' coursin' match he pulled off
wiv his cocks an' his hounds ; but there was
a chap came oot o' Aadcastle who was one
too many for him at the finish. This chap
had made a vast o' brass i' the toon at ship-
buildin' or such like, an' bein' wishful to set
hisself up as a big pot, had hired a big place
next grandfeythor's i' the country. Well,
grandfeythor couldn't abide him, for, bein' a
red-hot Tory, he didn't believe i' one man
bein' as good as another at aal, an' when, as
happened shortlies, his neighbour's son came

* Northumberland Plate, or Pitmen's Derby.

sweetheartin' his daughter, he says, "No Crozier lass ever yet married a shopkeeper's son, an' they never shall as long as I'm above ground—orffice boys mun marry wi' orffice gals," says he.

'Well, the lad's feythor was tarr'ble vext at this, an' he swears he'll have his revenge on the Squire—an' it wasn't long before he got his opportunity.

'He'd set hissel' up as a sportin' man, ye ken, when he come to the country, an' wes tarr'ble keen o' shootin' wiv a gun, an' occasionally he meets grandfeythor at a shootin' party, an' always takes the opportunity to differ from him i' a polite sort o' way on every topic under the sun.

'Well, after their dinners one day, grandfeythor, bein' fairly full up wi' beer, ye ken, begins sneering at all toon's folk settin' up as sportsmen. "It stan's to reason," says he, "if a man's forbears have never handled a gun, nor shot nowt mevvies* but a hoody

---

* 'Mevvies' = maybe, perhaps. The true Northumbrian is in a threefold danger of betraying his origin :

crow or a seagull on a holiday, that the bairns canna shoot either, for it's bred an' born in a man—it's part o' his birthright, like a fam'ly jool," says he ; "a heditary gift, the same as a proper knowledge o' horseflesh, fightin' cocks, greyhounds an' aal ; money won't buy it, an' it's no use argifyin' aboot it, for it's a fact, and the will o' Providence," says he.

'Noo, when grandfeythor got on aboot Providence, most folks, I b'lieve, used to say nowt, but Smithson—that was the chap's name—he gies a sort o' tee-hee at this oot loud, which would be the same as if you or me were to say, " It's just d——d nonsense."

'Well, there was a tarr'ble tow-row at this, grandfeythor as red as a bubbly-jock an' swearin' like a drunken fishwife, and Smithson as polite as a counter-jumper wiv his " pardon

phonetically, by the 'burr' ; dialectically, by constant use of 'mevvies,' 'wor' (our), and 'I's warned' (I warrant you) ; psychologically, by a perpetual readiness to back himself, his dog, or any of his belongings, against any other man's in the world, and for any amount, at a moment's notice.

me's" and "pray be seated, sirs"—aal to no effect.

'At the finish, when matters were quieted doon a bit, Smithson offers to back hissel' at a shootin' match wi' grandfeythor for £1,000 a side, an' also at a cockin' match—"a long main" it was to be—twenty battles at £100 the "battle" and £1,000 the "main."

'Well, aal the comp'ny thought it was just a bit swagger on the part o' Smithson, an' that when the time came he'd just cry off an' pay forfeit, for the match was to take place in three weeks' time, and never a cock had Smithson in his place ava, whereas grand-feythor, he had a rare breed, the best i' the county—mixed Rothbury an' Felton—an' the old Felton breed was the one the King o' England win his brass ower formerly.

'The time comes, an' the comp'ny is aal assembled i' the cock-pit at Bridgeton, grandfeythor, full o' beans an' bounce, backin' hissel' like a prize-fighter, takin' snuff an' handin' roon' the box to his friends, an' sayin' noo an' again, "Where's that dam' fellow Smithson ?"

'Well, the clock on the old tower was just on the stroke of ten, when in saunters Smithson, cool as a ha'penny ice, an' behind him, in green and gold liv'ries, come ten flunkies each wi' two big bags behind his shoulder, an' in each bag a tarr'ble fine fightin' cock.

'Where he'd gathered them nobody knew save old Ned Stevison—an ancient old cock-fighter o' Bridgeton, who loved cocks more than many a man his missus. "The Moonlight Breed" he called them, but they had a strain of the famous old Lord Derby's breed i' them, and were blood uns to the bone.

'Some half dozen were Stevison's own, but the remainder 'twas said he had stolen from awa doon Sooth for Smithson, an' any-ways "Captain Moonlight" was his nick-name ever afterwards.

'Well, they weighs aal the cocks ; from six

to six and a half pounds their weight was to be, an' the fight commences.

'Bob Stevison fought Smithson's cocks for him, an' grandfeythor fought his own, kneelin' doon on the cock-pit floor wiv his coat off so as to handle them the better.

'The first two or three battles grand-feythor wins easy, Stevison using his warst cocks at the first, d'ye see, oot o' craft mevvies to get longer odds i' the bettin', so that at one time grandfeythor was five battles to two to the good ; a bit later it was eight all, an' the excitement was im-mense, bets flyin' aboot like snowflakes at Christmas.

'Then Stevison oots wiv a beauty—a perfect picture it was ov a fighter ; eyes like a furnace at night, liftin' his legs like a Derby winner, wings an' tail clipped short—aal glossy wi' health an' shinin' like mahogany.

'Stevison runs him up an' doon the floor to heat his blood, an' tweaks a feather doon from his rump—that was a clever trick he

had, to madden his cock just before the start
—an' holds him ready for the battle.

' Then grandfeythor, he oots wiv his
champion cock—" Stingo," he called him—
an old favouryte ov his, a gran' bird too, six
years old, an' a little past his prime mevvies,
though he'd never lost a battle in his life.

' As soon as they sees each other " Stingo"
gies a bit triumphant crow, an' leans forward
from his master's hand to try an' nip hold o'
the other wiv his beak. The other says
nowt, just looks at him wi' fiery eyes red
hot wi' murder, an' as soon as ever his feet
touch the sawdust bends low, then springs
straight for Stingo, drivin' wiv his spur o'
shinin' steel right for his heart.

' Just i' the nick o' time Stingo leaps i' the
air to meet him; there's a "click, click,"
" click, click," as o' daggers crossin', an'
pantin' from the shock, doon sinks either bird
to the ground.

' Stevison's mouth was tremblin' like a
bairn's as he took his favouryte up, for there

was blood on his lower breast feathers, but
Stingo wasn't touched ava, an' grandfeythor,
puffed oot wi' pride, claps a bit mair o' the
fam'ly property on to his champion.

'It was a bit lesson for the other cock ; he
was just as determined as ever, but a bit
quieter like ; round an' round Stingo he goes
like a prize-fighter, clickin' in noo an' again
as he thought he saw his openin', an' when
they grappled tegither wi' their beaks, though
his comb was almost torn in two, he ham-
mered for Stingo's eye as a blacksmith
hammers on his anvil.

'After about fifteen minutes neither cock
could stand straight ; at a distance you'd
have said they was both as drunk as my
lord ; both were drippin' blood ; Stingo had
lost an' eye, an' neither o' t'other's were
much use to him, bein' bunged up wi' bruised
flesh.   They staggered aboot here an' there ;
knocked up against each other in a blind-
man's "beg-pardin" sort o' way.   Every noo
and again the Moonlight cock would pull

himself together, hop feebly into the air, an'
strike wiv his spurs, but as often as not the
air was all he hit, for, his eyesight bein' aal
askew, he couldn't aim straight, an' doon he
would flop on his tail end, coughin' an'
choakin' wi' blood—powerless, yet mad to
gan on fightin'.

'At the finish he gets Stingo pinned up
against the cockpit bars, an', thinkin' he has
him noo, gies a feeble craw, lifts hissel' into
the air, an' claps for his heart wiv his spurs.

'There was a bit clash in the held-breath
stillness of the place, then a tiny moan, an',
by Gox! there was Moonlight lyin' flat on his
back on the sawdust wiv one leg broke in two
an' danglin' wiv its spur like a watch-chain on
his breast.

'Such a hullaballoo as there was, grandfeythor yellin' like an Injun! "Pick up yo'r
bird," he cries, "he's a dead un!" for there
was Stingo a-top o' Moonlight peckin' at
what was left ov his head-piece like a black-
bird at a snail.

2

'Stevison never moved, but his gills went flutterin' like those ov a dyin' fish ; he couldn't speak, but I b'lieve he was prayin' for his favouryte.

'A minute passed, then Moonlight comes to ; he beats wiv his wings, struggles, crawls an inch or two, manages to shake off Stingo, then hoistin' hissel' up once again wiv his one leg an' wings slashes wiv his spur, and by the damn'dest luck lands it in Stingo's eye.

'Doon in a motionless heap they falls, an' when they're separated Stingo's dead as a leg o' mutton.

'The rest o' the comp'ny yells and shouts ; some says Moonlight's a dead un, too, an' it's a drawn battle, an' grandfeythor, he swears his bird can still fight, while Stevison, unable to find his voice, picks up Moonlight, an' finally claps a great kiss on to the middle ov his back, an' when he sets him doon again wiv a drop brandy in his mouth he sets up a feeble craw of defiance, plainly axin', " Who the deevil says I's a dead un ?"

'After that it was all up wi' grandfeythor; the stuffin' seemed knocked oot o' him an' his cocks by the loss ov his favouryte, an' in the next battle another of his best birds had his heart squashed oot, like a ripe gooseberry, at the vary first encounter.

'It was a black day that for grandfeythor, but, as I was sayin' at the start, he never gies in, an' he comforts hissel' wi' thinkin' he'd make matters square up an' a bit to spare by the shootin' match which was to follow in a fortnight's time.

'Smithson had agreed to shoot off the match at Crozier Hall, for grandfeythor had aboot the best shootin' in the county at the time, an' there was one place famous for the grand shots ye got overhead between two woods planted on either side of a dene, ye ken.

'There was stubbles an' beanfields usuallies beyond, an' the pheasants, when driven off, used to fly right across the haugh below over into the woods beyond—mevvies aboot two hundred yards awa'.

'Well, the great day comes. A fine, sunshiny October day it was, wiv a bit o' wind from the west—the way the birds was to fly, ye ken, an' a tarr'ble big comp'ny was assembled to see grandfeythor gie "the furrinor" his gruel.

'Grandfeythor was i' tremendous spirits that mornin', an' as full o' gob as a torkey-cock ; nothin' could hold him ; the world was a toy to him—like the geography chap* i' the bairns' books, ye ken—he felt sae tarr'ble strong an' healthy. " Eyeball clear as a bairn's," says he, "hand steady as a rock, digestion a marvel," an' he pats hissel' on the stomach as pleased as Punch.

'They tosses as to who shoots first, an' the coin comes doon for grandfeythor, an' mighty delighted he was to be the first to shoot. There wasn't much chance o' grandfeythor's bettin' as much as he wished for, for naebody thought Smithson had a chanst, but what he could get he gobbled up like a hungry trout—fearfu'

* Atlas, presumably.

odds they was—six to one on himself he had to lay, an' often a bit more.

'The match was for £1,000 a side, a hundred shots each at the first hundred pheasants within shot, an' the referee to decide any disputed points.

'Grandfeythor takes up his stand aboot thirty yards awa' from the wood's edge; then the referee fires a pistol, the head-beater i' the wood above waves a white flag, an' there's a dead stillness as though we were aal i' church prayin'.

'There was a big clump o' fir-trees standin' right oot from the thick o' the wood's edge about fifty yards off mevvies, an' two o' the firs stood oot high above their fellows, an' that was where the pheasants always broke oot, whizzin' up like rockets as they came ower the top o' them, an' it was just at that point that grandfeythor had always nicked them clever—just as they cleared the rise of the topmost tree, ye ken, an' started on their level flight for the opposite side. If ye missed them i' front ye hadn't much chanst behind, for they swept awa' like lightnin' doon the wind before ye could get turned round. Well, aal was stillness as I said, when sudden there comes a far-away cry through the clear air—"Cock forrard, cock forrard!" an' in another two seconds there comes a clap o' wings from above. Bang! gans grandfeythor's gun, as a fine cock sweeps overhead. "D——!" says he, wiv a flush on his cheek; for aal there was to show was some half-dozen tail feathers left twirlin', as if in mock'ry, forty yards in the air above him.

'"Cock forrard, cock forrard!" comes the cry again, an' grandfeythor grips a firmer stand wiv his feet, an' grasps his weapon a bit tighter than before. Bang, bang! this time, an' the cock gies a frightful lurch as though about to fall headlong, but steadies hissel', rises a bit, an' wins over to the other side.

'"H——!" yells grandfeythor, trembling

wi' rage, an' stamps upon the ground. "Cock forrard, cock forrard!" again comes the beater's cry, an' half a dozen come flightin' overhead at once.

'Bang! once again, an' grandfeythor wiv a groan flings his gun to the ground, for he had missed altogether that time.

'"I'm fair bewitched," he cries, and aal the while the pheasants were streamin' overhead.

'He trembled aal over, an' we thought he was gannin' to have a fit, for his brow was damp wi' drops o' sweat, an' his eye wild an' glassy. "Thoo damned fellow," he cries, glancing round at Smithson, an' takes a step towards him, "thoo's cozened me somehow, thoo must have poisoned my beer!" he yells.

'"Steady, sir, for God's sake, steady!" says the keeper in his ear, an' offers him his gun again ready loaded for another shot, for aal the while the pheasants came liftin' above their heads.

'Well, he takes it up again, looks at it an'

feels as though he didn't recognise it, as though it had injured him somehow, an', tremblin' aal over, takes up a stand again. After a shot or two he kills one in beautiful style, an' gradually getting back a bit o' confidence he gets warmed up, an' at the finish he has seventy-five oot o' the hundred —oot o' the last twenty never missin' one.

'And noo it was Smithson's turn.

'He makes a splendid start, wipin' up the first fifteen birds wivvoot an error; after that again the pheasants come wilder, an' gettin' flurried belike, he tailors them. Then he gets steadied once more, an' at the finish has ten cartridges left an' seventy birds doon.

'A wunnerfu' chap for nerve he was, was Smithson; the mair excitement the cooler he gets.

'A hen pheasant comes sailin' awa' to the right some sixty yards off.

'"In shot?" asked he, as though he were passin' the time o' day.

'"Shoot," cries the referee, an' ping, ping!

gans two cartridges, but he cannot stop her, she was ower far off, though she left a trail o' feathers ahint her.

'He gets another fearfu' hard one to the left this time, an' it takes two cartridges to settle number seventy-one—six cartridges left an' five birds to bag.

'Wow! but the excitement was painfu', an' folks fell to bettin' i' quick whispers, "Two to one against Smithson," an' he takes it wiv a nod, smilin' if you please.

'The next three he gets, then he misses a longish shot, two cartridges left an' two birds to knock doon.

'Here they come—two cocks high together overhead—be-eauties; suthin' seems wrang wi' trigger or cartridge, an' Smithson misses first barrel.

'"I've won!" yells grandfeythor, an' tosses his cap i' the air. Bang! says Smithson's second barrel, an' doon comes the two cock pheasants togither. The first had swerved, d'ye see, an' jostled up against the second,

an' Smithson cops 'em both wiv his last
cartridge an' wins on the post, seventy-six to
seventy-five. Gox ! but it was the nearest
touch an' go thing ever seen i' the North
Country, I's warn'd, an' wi' that last cartridge
bang gans Crozier Hall.'

'Was there any trickery ?' I inquired ; 'had
Smithson tampered with your grandfather's
cartridges, for instance ?'

'No, he'd not done that ; he couldn't ha'
done that, but he had tricked grandfeythor a
bit, though it wasn't found out till afterwards.

'The way of it was this : Smithson was a
d——d clever feller, ye ken, an' knowin' as
he did that grandfeythor had a wunnerfu'
way o' pickin' off the pheasants just as they
came over the topmost trees, he had sent two
or three o' his men i' the night-time, an' had
fixed up a young fir right on to the top o' the
highest tree, so that Mr. Pheasant had to rise
another six feet afore he cam' ower.

'Well, this was just enough to put grandfeythor oot ov his reckonin's, an' when he

misses the first one, as he'd never done before, he cannot make it oot, he went clean flustered, thought he must have had a stroke, an' swore he was bewitched, or poisoned, or such like.

'It was a crool thing to do, but it wasn't exactly what ye could call a Jew's swindle— but, damn Smithson aal the same, I says ; for here's me, Geordie Crozier, left a po'r orphin i' the warld wi' none o' his fam'ly property to belang to him, 'cept two gifts— the yen for drinkin' an' t'other for gamblin', an' it's damn Smithson, says I.'

THE SQUIRE'S LAST RIDE

'AY, that's the priest, the Catholic Priest,' said Eph Milburn, after a white-haired, cassock-clad old gentleman, who had nodded slightly in reply to my companion's greeting, had passed over the bridge and departed out of hearing.

'He looks as if butter wouldn't melt in his mouth now,' continued Milburn, a long-legged, ruddy-bearded, hawk-eyed son of the moorlands, 'and aal his time nowadays he spends in his garden over his bees or his flowers, or thumbing his Mass-book in his library; but it wasn't so once-a-day, not he, not when the old Squire was above ground, and he came up by to stop wiv him.

'Ye'll have heard tell o' the old Squire an'

aal his goin's on, I'll be bound? Ay, o'
course, but there's one thing nobody kens o',
not even Father Blenkinsop, and that's where
the Squire's bones are lyin', for they never
found his body, ye ken.

'Squire Dally was the last o' the fam'ly
that had lived in the old Pele Tower o' Dally
from generation to generation, and he was
the wildest o' a wild lot —riders an' reivers
in the old times, canny hard fox-hunters,
drinkers, an' gam'lers this century. They
were bound to get through their property
soon or late, an' the last Squire, Tom Dally
o' Dally, he says, "I leave my property tiv
a South-countryman? Not I, by Gad!" says
he; "why, damme, but I'll cheat him yet,"
an' sae he spends hissel' right an' left on any
mortal thing he took a fancy for.

'The Hall—which was an old Pele wi'
two wings added, ye ken—an' a good bit o'
the property, had gone before that. The
last Squire's grandfeythor had got shot o'
that, the mortgages on it bein' far ower

heavy to keep up; but there was still a fair
property left, an' a nice canny house that had
once been a dower-house, an' was now a
farm, an' that was where Squire Tom lived
with his fighting-cocks, an' his hounds, an'
his hawks an' aal.

'His missus had died early, ye ken, an'
that had been the ruin ov him, for she was
a clivvor woman, wiv a turn o' management
—just what ye would call good hands i' the
matter ov a horse; that was her faculty, an'
she was a bonny-featured woman for-bye.

'Ay, she could manage him fine.

'There was a grand scene, 'twas always
said, when he brings her home after their
furrin' tower, an' one night, bein' merry wiv
his bottle, he forgets hissel', an' swears at
her before company. Up she gets swiftly,
pale, but determined, an' leanin' a wee bit
ower the table she speaks straight at him.
"Tom," she says, "you forget yourself; and
until you apologize to me for your rudeness
I'll sit no more at table wi' ye," an' oot she

gans frae the dining-room, haughty as the
Queen in Scripture, leavin' the Squire gapin'
an' speechless, never havin' been treated that
fashion before.

'There was two or three other men wiv
him dinin' that night, an' on they sat drinkin'
steadily, the Squire in a towerin' temper aal
the while, noo damnin' hissel', next cursin'
his neighbour, an' backin' his horses, an'
hawks, an' hissel', wi' gun an' rod, against
anyone, or the lot o' them together.

'They tried to soothe him a bit, but the
mair they tried the hotter he got, an' had the
Pope hissel' been his visitor that night,
Squire Tom would have d——d him too, an'
been glad o' the opportunity. After a bit
mair snarlin', an' sneerin', an' snappin', he
sits quiet for a while, then he glares round at
his guest friends, an' he cries :

' " Ye're nowt better than a lot o' 'momenty
morries,' "—meanin' skeletons, ye ken—"the
wife's worth the whole boilin' o' ye, an' I'm
d——d if I don't apologize," an' he glared

round to see if anyone would dare laugh at him for't; but no one spoke save a little fam'ly lawyer chap, up for the night frae the toon, an' he chirrups up an' he says, "Qui' right, qui' right," he hiccoughs, an' the Squire glares right through him as he growls, "When I ask ye for an opinion I pay ye for't, but if ye advise me unasked again, I'll fling ye oot at window," he says.

'Sae oot he strides into the hall, an' cries up the stairs: "Nell, my lass, Nell, ho-way doon, an' I'll apologize to ye, ay, d——, I will," an' doon she comes, an' on tiv his knees he gans, an' she holds oot her hand, an' the Squire he kisses it like a lover.

'Well, she manages him clivvor, but in her first child-bed she was taken ill, poor lady, an' dies vary shortly, leavin' him wiv a baby girl.

'After that the Squire was never the same man again. He turned reckless, for what was the use ov "a filly" to him, he says; an'

havin' no son an' heir to live an' save for, he
sets hissel' to spend aal he can an' spite his
next o' kin—a barrister chap in London toon,
whom he hated for bein' no sportsman—"a
priest-faced, pauper chap iv a black gown an'
wig," he called him, an' no love was lost
between the pair o' them.   He was a good
bit older than the Squire, an' had a largish
fam'ly, the second son bein' none other than
Father Blenkinsop—the priest that's just
passed us by.

'He was the only one the Squire could
take up wi' at aal, an' as a boy he was often
there for shootin', an' huntin', an' fishin',
though his father liked ill his bein' there, for
fear o' his gettin' into bad ways under the
Squire's guidance, who was gettin' wilder an'
wilder wiv every year that passed.   He was
just a boy then, was Father Blenkinsop,
havin' left his schoolin', an' bein' aboot to
gan tiv a college to be turned into a Jesu-yte,
an' nowt pleased the Squire mair, after a long
day's huntin' or hawkin', than to fill the lad

up wi' liquor an' sneer at religion, an' Mass,
an' priests, an' aal.

'"Chuck it, my boy, chuck it," he would
say, clappin' him on the shoulder, as he
passed the bottle about. "Divv'nt put on
the black petticoat; ye're ower much ov a
man for that. Ye can ride, an' ye can
shoot, an' ye can look a gal i' the face, an'
ye can crack a bottle, but if ye turn priest,
ye'll neither be man nor woman, but a ——
bad mixture o' both."

'So he would talk o' nights, pourin' oot
his ribaldries an' drinkin' doon his wine, yet
never gettin' fair drunk; for he had a marvel-
lous stomach for liquor, had the Squire—no
butt o' Malmsey wine could ever have
drooned him, I's warn'd—an' the only way
he betrayed himself was by gettin' a bit
hotter i' the face an' fiercer i' his talk.

'Well, one night he vexed his young
cousin beyond bearin'—what wi' black-
guardin' his father an' his mother, an' wi'
one thing an' another—an' sudden the boy

leaps up—mevvies he was a little above hissel' wi' liquor that evenin'—an' he bangs wiv his fist on the table, an' he cries, " Look here, Cousin Tom, I'll stand it no longer, an' to prove I'm no coward, I'll challenge ye to ride to the big Black Stone on Glowrorum Fell an' back across the Moor this very night."

'" Done wi' ye, lad, done wi' ye !" shouts the Squire, bangin' wiv his fist in his turn, "an' I'll tell ye what the stakes shall be.   If I win, you chuck the Jesu-yte business an' come an' live wi' me, an' if you win, you can take your pick o' the horses i' my stable. Agreed ?"

'" Ay !" shouted the boy recklessly ; "done wi' ye."

' Fifteen minutes after this the two o' them starts off with a wild hallo up the brae side, an' so across the Moor, the Squire "yoickin'"' an' "tally-hooin'"' as he went.

' The Moor was mevvies aboot two miles across—an' a tarr'ble bad place for hard gallopin', for there was a stone wall or two i' the middle o't, bogs to the left hand, an' some old workin's—pit-shafts or the like— to the right.

'So right across Towlerhirst Moor they galloped—hell-to-leather—the Squire to the right an' the boy to the left.

'Tom Brewis, the old herd up at Windy-neuk, happened to be passin' along the sheep-track that leads by the Moor edge that night, an' hearin' the sound ov a horse gallopin', an' a lively hollerin' as tho' to a pack o' hounds, he comes across a bit to find oot what it might be.

'It was a dampish, daggyish sort o' night, but at times there was a drift o' moonlight, an' in one o' thae glimpses he caught a sight ov a dark figure on horseback, aboot two hundred yards from him, tryin' to jump a big black horse across one o' thae open shafts. "You won't, won't you? Then d—— ye, ye —— black de'il, ye shall!" an' clappin' his spurs deep into his sides, an'

layin' his huntin' crop aboot his ears, he
forced him some paces backward an' sent
him at it again.

'It was a big black stallion he was ridin'—
a fiery-tempered brute, a proper match for
the Squire—an' up he reared on end, fightin'
him, shriekin' wi' pain an' rage ; but he
couldn't get shot ov his rider, so wiv a
sudden bound he starts forward an' tries to
clear the shaft wiv one great leap.

'Just at that moment the moonlight faded,
an' Tom Brewis couldn't tell exactly what
happened, but he saw a dark mass leapin',
he heard a rattle o' stones, then a heavy thud
deep down somewhere, a sort o' splash, an'
aal was still.

'Tom stands there aal a-gliff wi' terror,
half dazed, not kennin' whether he can have
seen or heard aright ; then, pullin' hissel'
together, walks slowly thither to see if any
trace can be seen of horse or rider.

'But there wasn't a one—neither o' horse
nor Squire—nowt but a tramplin' o' horse's

hoofs an' a white gash as o' a half horse-shoe
on a big boulder o' rock two feet below the
surface t'other side. Sae Tom gans slowly
back, an' doon to the Squire's house to find
if he can hear anything ov him doon there;
for he half hoped it might be a sort o' dream
after aal.

'Just as he gets to the door a figure comes
up the drive leadin' to the house, draggin'
a lame horse after him, an' "Ha' ye seen
anything o' the Squire?" it shouts at him.
"No-o," says Tom, startled-like, "that was
just what I was comin' to ask for myself;"
an' he peers through the shadows to see who
his questioner could be, an' recognises Master
Fred, the Squire's cousin, bleedin' frae a
wound i' the head, an' leadin' a horse wi' two
fearfu' broken knees.

'He win his wager,' concluded my companion slowly, 'but after that ride he was
never the lad he had been before, an' perhaps
it's scarcely likely that he should be, I'm
thinkin'.'

A L'OUTRANCE

WE were standing on the fencing-room floor—Jake Carruthers and I—leaning our backs against the armoury, our foils still in our hands, slowly recovering our breath, after a rapier and dagger contest which had lasted a good half-hour.

He was much less 'winded' than myself, for all his sixty-five years ; and as I had positively worn myself out against his iron wrist I was delighted to gain a breathing space, and occupied the time in drawing out from my companion some old-time memories of the fencing floor.

'Have you ever seen a duel ?' I inquired. 'I don't mean a semi-drunken, nose-chopping bout, or a garden-party affair, with coffee and liqueurs, as in France, but a genuine " throat-cutting, blood-letting " matter, such as Porthos or D'Artagnan would have loved ?'

' No,' replied Jake reflectively, drawing the length of his foil lovingly along the soft sleeve of his jacket; " the time's past, I doubt, for that sort of performance. The Divorce Court is what " my lord " appeals to nowadays for " satisfaction," and Trimmer Joe or Bricklayer Tom, they just " bash " the trespasser upon their family preserves on the head, and there's an end on't.

' The cleverest, best-fought fight I ever saw—and I believe there was a bit something of what you're meanin' in it—was, strange to say, twixt a man and a woman— leastways, a gentleman an' a lady. It was a fair battle, proper fightin' on her side ; for she was sworn to win, and sair wishful to punish him, I's warn'd ; and he, though he was tarr'ble keen to win too, found it took him all his time to keep her from letting daylight into him—an', by the way, this is the varra tale ye used always to be askin' for, an' I'll tell it ye noo, for ye've improved i' your fencin', I'm thinkin', since ye began. You'll have heard tell of Squire Dennington of Dennington Hall? A great rider he was once, and a sportsman generally—"Jockey Jack" his own private friends called him, and his horse, "Pit Laddie"—ye'll heard of him? —won the "Plate" some thirty years back.

'Well, his lady, Mrs. Dennington, was just the proudest woman in the whole county of Northumberland—scarcely what ye would call "bonny," but just tarr'ble handsome, and the Squire, he fair worships her. He had married her in Berlin, and there was some queer odds an' ends o' stories about her, but he'd never have hearkened to the many more than he would listen to anyone shoutin' to him the way to go out hunting.

'He was in the army at that time, ye ken —the Northumberland Fusiliers, "The Old and Bold," with "Where the Fates calls ye"

in Latin for their motto—and I was his man-
servant, joining the army along of him, as my
forbears had often done with his forbears
beforetime.

‘ The Squire had to go out to Berlin with
his mother, and he gets leave for me to
accompany him, and there it was that he
met with his lady that was to be—Miss
Maxwell as she was then.

‘ She was the handsomest woman in Berlin,
’twas said, but quite poor, living as a companion with the wife of one of the Ambas-
sador's party, being a kind of cousin, and
many were the stories about her.

‘ Gossip said that one of them grand dukes
with a name a yard long had wanted her for
his mistress, but when he made his proposi-
tion he got such an answer that he never
dared speak to her again.   Then it was
reported that she was engaged to the Ambas-
sador's chief secretary, Oxencourt his name
was—Sir Henry Oxencourt as he is now—and
that she had even run away with him, but

that at the last moment he turned round and said that he couldn't afford to marry her till his father died, so there and then she leaves him, walks the night through till she can get a conveyance, and arrives just in time to stay the mouth of scandal from ruining her reputation.

'Well, the Squire meets her, falls desperately into love—for he cares nothing for gossips—and in three weeks' time she accepts him for good and all.

'They marries at once, and travel for a year or more, and finally settle down at Dennington Hall.

'The Squire after a bit sends for me, buys my discharge, makes me his body-servant, and sets up the old banqueting-room as a fencing hall—for he was always tarr'ble keen at fencing, boxing, single-stick, and all manly sports—and it was part of my duty to give them both a turn of fencing most mornings of the week.

'Well, one winter, after about three years

of marriage, the Squire goes off to Algeria to shoot gazelle, leaving Mrs. Dennington and his sister behind at the Hall, and he hadn't been gone more than a week before Sir Henry Oxencourt turns up at the Hall.

'Well, when I see him there, I was fair dismayed, for I kenned nicely there was but one thing he could be wantin', for his repute in the matter of women was notorious. Forbye that ancient gossip at Berlin had always reported that he had been mad at missing his chance with her, and had sworn he would win her back again—get her a divorce and marry her himself at the finish.

'His father had died since then, and he was now a rich man, and as handsome and masterful a man as ever I saw in my life.

'Well, he comes and he courts her the live-long day, quiet-like and respectful, but never missing an opportunity, and she seems to enjoy his company. They go out hunting together ; she dares him to jump this and he dares her to jump that, and so the play goes on, and all the while I was fearing he was getting a fast hold upon her, for she liked power and was tarr'ble ambitious, and Sir Henry, they said, might have been one of the cleverest diplomatists in the world if he could but have kept clear of women.

' It was easy to see that he was just mad keen for her, but I was not so sure after a bit that she was so keen for him. It seemed to me she was leading him on, and leading him on, but with what purpose I couldn't guess.

' Well, one afternoon she comes to me and she says, off-hand like, " Sir Henry Oxencourt would like to show me some new tricks of fence he has learnt abroad ; kindly see that the fencing-room is in order to-night, and, by the way, I want to show him the pair of duelling rapiers, with the silver foxes on the hilts, that Mr. Dennington is so fond of."

' Well, all afternoon I wondered what it meant ; for though her manner was cool enough, there was something curious about my mistress's expression as she gave her orders.

'"If possible," I thinks to myself, "I'll have a peep also at Sir Henry's tricks to-night," and as I polished up the rapiers that afternoon I thought of the story the Squire used to tell of them. One of them had a stain on the "foible" which would not come out for any quantity of rubbing—it was the blood, the Squire said, of a certain "Black Rutherford," who had made love to the then Lady Dennington when her Knight was away fighting for King Charlie. Sir John comes back, having heard about it, but says nothing, and asks him to dinner; they have a game of cards after; Sir John accuses him of cheating, and there and then in the banqueting-hall they have a set-to with their rapiers before my lady's eyes; in five minutes Sir John disarms him, and before the rapier touches the floor, runs him clean through the right lung and out below the shoulder-blade.

'Well, after taking in coffee that evening,

I went to the fencing-room, and on the pretence of looking after the fire, mending jackets, straightening masks, and so forth, stayed on there till about ten o'clock, when in comes Mrs. Dennington, followed by Sir Henry.

'She gives a sort of start when she sees me, then she says curtly, "You needn't stay, Carruthers," and walks past me into the middle of the room.

'Well, I felt bound to see that fencing, whatever it might be, and the only way I could manage it was to go round and up to the old musicians' gallery at the southern end. If I could open the door without attracting notice, I might then lie down at full length and see pretty well what was going on below.

'It took me the best part of five minutes to open the door and squeeze through, and when I had crawled to the ledge and looked over, the two combatants were just about to begin.

4

' " Put the letters on the mantelpiece," I could hear her say with a curiously strung tone to her voice, and Sir Henry bowed in a mocking sort of way. Then he says slowly, after having walked to the chimney-piece and placed a packet on the shelf : " But it is not quite fair, of course, for you cannot see your stakes, whereas I—I have mine before my eyes at the end of my blade —the most beautiful stakes in Europe," and he bowed again to Madame with an air of gallantry and passion and arrogance all in one.

' For reply the mistress only gave a quick nod with her head, nervous, impatient, like a racehorse that must be away.

' I daren't do more than peep over now and again, for the lights were bright below, and I was afraid of being caught ; but I could see that she was in a state of great excitement, while he was cool in comparison with her, and wore a proud, triumphing sort of air, as of one who knows full well he has the victory in his grasp.

'They walk to the centre of the hall and take their stands. They "take length," and then salute—she, swiftly, nervously, he in a foreign, bravado sort of fashion.

'"First blood," says Sir Henry, "and the stakes are won," saluting once again in a vainglorious way he had.

'"Yes, but not for a scratch," replies my lady swiftly. Then they cross rapiers, and the play begins.

'My sangs! but it wasn't a play at all, it was a reg'ler battle, a fair duello, and it was all Sir Henry could do to hold his own. They had engaged in "quatre," and no sooner had blades touched than she disengages and feints in "tierce"; then, with an amazing swiftness, she disengages again, and lunges full at him in "sixte"; carelessly he parries with "sixte," and in a flash she disengages again, "beats" his blade downwards, and, for all but a biscuit, has him disarmed. He loses hold of his weapon, his fingers slipping from the quillons, but

4—2

catches it in mid-air before it drops, leaps back a yard, parrying another lunge clever with his left hand as he does so.

'"'Tis a dirty Italian trick ye have learnt! they haven't improved ye abroad!" my lady sneers at him.

'Now, had she been but one flash of an eye quicker with her lunge after the "beat," she'd have had him in "quatre" nicely, but she hadn't thought she could disarm him so easy, and she just missed her chance. Sir Henry, though, had had his lesson; he drops his careless, tempting manner, such as a professor tries a beginner with, and fights cooler and more careful, chucking his bravado airs, for it's dead in earnest she is, and no mere stage-play for the gallery.

'On she comes again like a tigress, evidently trying to "rush" him, and back and back she presses him till the pair o' them's right under the gallery where I was lying. I had my head right through the bars by that time, I was so keen to see the fight, and it was only by stuffing my handkerchief into my mouth that I could stop myself from shouting advice and encouragement to her, she fought so desperate keen and with such a wild-cat pluck.

'It wasn't exactly scientific, her fencing, it was too rash and all-for-victory straight away, but it was grand to see her flashing her rapier in and out, flickering like a serpent's tongue, and all the while her graceful limbs moved softly, swiftly, like a panther's, beneath her silken evening dress.

'Once Sir Henry's foot slipped, and in she comes like a knife, and he only escapes by adopting another Italian trick—that of dropping with the left hand to the floor. She still presses him harder than ever, and I could hear her breathing hotly, "heck, heck," like an angered hawk. Then swift he "binds" with her, but he does it over-viciously and pays for it, for she's agile as a cat, and freeing herself with a leap backward, suddenly with a lightning-like "cut-over" touches him on the sword arm, and though he wouldn't acknowledge it, I knew she'd pricked him, and I could tell that it had roused him to anger in his turn. "You she-devil!" I heard him hiss between his teeth, and now he turned to the offensive himself.

'He was at a disadvantage, though, for he didn't want to hurt her badly, being a woman, so he tries to disarm her, and give her some slight wound on the sword arm, or high in "quatre" or "tierce."

'That was no good, as I could have told him nicely, for she had the strongest and supplest wrist of any woman ever I saw, and forbye that, disarming can only be done by taking your opponent unawares, and she kenned nicely what he was after.

'Then sudden he gies it up, seeing the uselessness o't, and tries a brute strength game, waits his chance till he can lift up her blade, and then thrusts sideways so as to pink her high in the shoulder, but she twists

aside and it only just touches her through
the sleeve. "First blood!" he shouts
triumphantly, "the stakes are mine," with
a low bow and a sweep o' the sword arm.
"Phit!" she cries passionately; "it's only a
scratch," and she comes again at him with a
bound.

'Then he loses his temper a bit, I think,
for his own sword arm was bleeding, as I
knew well, for I saw a drop or two of blood
on the floor and his hand was crimson
forbye. So he comes to meet her, quickly
driving her back in turn, plying his rapier
this way and that fiercely, just missing her
by a hair's breadth to frighten her, till he
could have her at his mercy, and then he
tries a "cut-over" in "tierce," swift as a
meteor, pressing his "fort" strongly against
her "foible," and would have been home
sure as fate had not his foot slipped on a
drop of blood on the floor. Up flies his
rapier idly—she with a sudden flip tosses it
higher still, and with a leap, by Gox! she

ran him through in "seconde"—just above his right hip.

'"Hurroo!" shouts I, through my handkerchief and all. "Clever, clever!" for it was splendidly done—scientific, exact, just perfection.

'There Sir Henry lay in a swoon upon the floor, for no doubt the pain and the shock together would be immense, while my mistress, she just takes one look at him, then wipes her rapier swift upon her handkerchief, takes up Sir Henry's also, and places them against the rack in the armoury, takes down two foils, throws one on the floor, breaks the other in two and flings the pieces down beside its fellow. Then swift as ever she goes to the mantelpiece, takes up the bundle of letters and chucks them into the fire.

'She watches them burn for a moment, then presses the electric bell close by, and just as John the footman walks in at the door Sir Henry comes to himself, and lifts himself up on to his elbow off the floor.

"Help Sir Henry Oxencourt up to his

room," says she, cool as a cucumber, "and tell Carruthers to attend to him, and to send for the doctor, if necessary. A foil broke as we fenced, and Sir Henry, I fear, has suffered through the accident."

'John stares with an open mouth, but a peremptory " Don't you understand?" from his mistress wakes him up, and he goes and helps Sir Henry up, who therewith slowly rises, and, resting one hand on John's shoulder, without one word limps away.

'The door shuts, and Mistress Dennington turns slowly to the fire, her eyes glued to them letters burning blackly amongst the coals. As she watches she takes a cigarette from a box on the mantelshelf, lights it, and I heard her say to herself, " You fool!" then she smokes a puff or two and again she says, "You fool!" and therewith taps her foot smartly on the floor.'

'But what do you think she meant by "fool"?' I here interrupted.

'Well,' replied Jake slowly, 'I've often asked myself that very question, and what I believe she meant was something o' this sort: "Fool not to take your chance—and such a chance!—when you had it, and Fool again, for not knowing me better than to think that of me when 'twas too late."'

'And now one more question,' I said, for Jake was preluding with his weapon once again, evidently anxious to commence another bout. 'Did you ever tell the Squire?'

'No, not exactly,' replied he, 'but I gave him a hint, and bank-notes wouldn't have bought that rapier after that, and there it still hangs in Dennington Hall in the armoury, I believe, though I haven't been there since the Squire died and I set up as a Maître d'Armes in Oldcastle here. The mistress, though, she's still alive, but she never cared for Northumberland—"so dull," says she, and goes and diverts herself in London town. And now no more talk. Gardez-vous, M'sieur—en garde, s'il vous plaît,' and with a smile he struck my foil upon the floor.

'T'OWD SQUIRE'

'NO, I never saw him, not the old Squire — "t'owd Squire," as they called him; but grandfather, he was thick with him, bein' the oldest farmer in the dale an' pretty nigh a gentleman hisself in those days; he was master of the 'ounds, d'ye see, when they was a trencher-fed pack—that was before Squire Heron took them over to t' new kennels at The Ford.

'Well, I done some pretty fair jumps myself at one time an' another in t' ring or steeple-chasin', but 'twas nowt to what he done, not even when a mare I was ridin' jumped over a wall an' fifteen feet into t' quarry t' other side.

'There's a pretty tidy place at t' bottom o'

that field'—pointing to a low-lying, marshy
expanse on the left that rose at the end to a
high bank—'that he jumped one afternoon
in cold blood which five out of six wouldn't
have touched in warm, but at t' end of his
time he was reckless—almost to touch on
madness, so grandfather always said. But if
ye'll bide here three minutes till I've seen the
mare looked to properly I'll tell ye a tale of
t' Squire—same as grandfather told it me.'

So saying Jack Skelton cantered round to
the farm, where he was now employed as
horse-breaker and showyard rider, while I
strolled down to view the leap at the end of
the field till he was free to join me. I could
see The Ford opposite to me as I walked
along—a square keep flanked with castel-
lated wings rising proudly amongst its trees
beyond the winding river in a circle of fir-
clad hills.

'The old Squire's' daughter lived there
now with her husband, who had taken her
name on his marriage, but they were child-

less, and the ancient race of Herons seemed destined to become extinct.

Arrived at the bank I saw a formidable gulf open below me, with a soft and rotten landing on the further side, some fourteen feet across, the space between oozy with marsh mud and choked drains. ' "All hope abandon ye who enter here," ' I quoted aloud, just as Jack Skelton came up to me.

'Ay,' he chuckled, 'it would be a job for a contractor to get a horse an' man out o' that, an' after that I'll lay odds but the laundry-maid would give her notice.

' It was a great big, seventeen hands horse he had that he jumped it with—an ugly devil to look at, light roan in colour, but up to any weight an' absolutely fearless. All ye had to do, as grandfather used to say, was to lay t' reins on his neck, and straight across country he'd go like a bird.

' He hadn't always been such a fierce one to go, hadn't t' Squire, and what changed his temper was what I was goin' to tell ye.

'There was a woman in it, d'ye see, an' that woman his wife. When first they was married no couple in broad Yorkshire was happier, as folk thought. She was a handsome lass and clever at book-larnin' an' suchlike, ambitious, too, like the clever ones usually are; but at first she was all for sport an' huntin', same as t'owd Squire, and where he went she mostly followed him, bein' as well mounted as himself. As for t'owd Squire, he was t' happiest man alive in those days—used to slap grandfather on t' back an' cry, after a steaming run, t' fox's mask in his hand ready to tie on to his missus's saddle, "By ——, Skelton, but she's the straightest woman rider in England, whether in or out o' t' shires."

'Yet for all that his happiness was short-lived, for after a son was born to him Mistress Heron seemed to lose heart for huntin' — her narves, she said, had gone wrong with her; but grandfather always upheld that she'd grown tired of her husband. She was a clever woman, as I said, an' ambitious; an' 'twas reported that she'd been forced to marry wi' t'owd Squire by her mother in Lunnon town—he bein' as rich as "Creases"—whilst the man she really favoured hadn't a penny beyond what his wits might bring him in. For a bit the excitement of huntin' had been enough for her, an' spendin' t' Squire's brass, t' big house, an' t' novelty; but after t' son was born she grew dissatisfied an' took a dislike to her life. Consequence was that she took up with a young man called Cunliffe, that lived over at The Tower—right away on that hillside over there, about two miles west of us—ye can see it against trees from Heronsford easy.

'The place had been bought by his father, who made money in trade at Ironopolis, an' he'd just got himself elected into Parliament, an' was like to get on at it, 'twas said, bein' one of them ready-witted, oily-tongued chaps that never go quite straight, but gallop along t' roads an' sneak through gates, an' then swagger on at t' kill. Ay, there's none "who-oops" an' "tally-hos" louder than them.

'T'owd Squire, on t'other hand, was one of t' owd-fashioned sort, and said what he meant always, an' clapped an oath on t' back of it; hated Lunnon, an' Lunnon ways, lived for huntin' an' shootin' an' country pursuits, an' drank a bottle of port wine reg'lar every evenin' to his own cheek. He wasn't over well educated neither, havin' all his life lived almost entirely at home; no scholar savin' a vast knowledge of the stud-book, farriery, an' horse-breedin', which was a sort o' larnin' that Mistress Heron didn't care a button about. Well, things went gradually askew between the two, she always wantin' fresh company in t' house, an' him hatin' society ways like poison.

'Amongst others she took up with was this young Member o' Parliament, Cunliffe, an' often he would be over an' dinin' with

them; he could sing a bit, an' she was fond
of t' piano, an' they would play on together
in t' drawing-room while t' Squire sat over
his mahog'ny passin' t' bottle round, talkin'
over t' 'untin', layin' wagers with his own
particular cronies of the red-faced, good-
hearted, rough-tongued, fox-'untin' Yorkshire
style.

'Well, t'owd Squire couldn't stomach
young Cunliffe at all; for in the first place
he was a poor rider to 'ounds, never jumped
owt if he could help it, was a mean chap
with his brass, an' had a supercilious way
o' talk about him that angered t' Squire
fearful. Add to this that he was always
comin' over to sweetheart his missus, an'
you can imagine how ill the two men would
agree.

'Well, one night they was sitting playin'
cards after dinner, an' Mistress Heron was
lookin' on at them. T' Squire was nowt of
a scholar, as I said before, but he had a good
head for cards, an' loved to take t' shekels

5

off young Cunliffe, who hated losin', but was generally the one who had to pay up.

'It was a game they call Pickit they were playin'; grandfather told me—for in after days t' Squire let out a good bit of his troubles to my grandfather, havin' been play-mates together, an' grandfather bein' a god-child o' t'owd Squire's father beside that— an' Cunliffe bein' flustered had forgot when it came to t' last two cards—there bein' a ticklish bit at stake—what had been played previously.

'He looked this way and that, then all of a sudden he catches Mistress Heron's eye, sees something in it that tells him somewhat, claps doon t' right card an' wins.

'T'owd Squire, he keeps extraordinary quiet, just gives one swift look round under his eyelids at his wife standin' there above him, an' says softly, "Ye've a wonderful memory, Mr. Cunliffe," says he, at which the other gets very red, an' begins to talk of getting home.

'"Mistress Heron and I," says t' Squire,
"were talking on this afternoon about t'
private steeplechase we're going to hold
shortly in t' Park here, an' she was all for
layin' out t' course for first two miles straight
west till it almost touches Towers gates. 'It
will just take inside of ten minutes from t'
Ford,' says she, 'to Towers turn, and beautiful going all the way over grass with t' big
jump an' t' black beck in t' middle of it.'
'Ay,' says I, 'and that will stop one or
two that I know of—I'll lay a monkey.'
'Not a bit of it,' says she, 'not a bit; an'
I'll take evens with ye that everybody
tries it.'

'"Now, as Mistress Heron is going to
ask ye to ride one of her nominations for her
at the race, it might be helpful to ye to have
a preliminary trial, an' as t' night is bright as
day wi' moonlight, perhaps ye'd like a ride
home to-night across country, an' I'll lay ye
double of what ye've won to-night that ye
don't get to your own gate-ends in, say,

twelve minutes from t' Ford's paddock. An' ye can have your pick o' what's in my stable," adds t' Squire, as he looks from one to t' other of them, "while Mistress Heron an' I will watch ye from t' battlements an' take time for ye; or, of course, if ye're afraid," he adds, as Cunliffe, hemming an' hawing, says something about "not likin' to take a horse out at that time o' night," an' dwells heavy on the words, "we can send ye home in the landau, like a lady," says t' Squire.

'"If Mr. Cunliffe accepts your proposal to ride a horse for me in the steeplechase," interrupts Mistress Heron scornfully, "that is of itself sufficient to falsify your insinuation."

'"I shall be only too proud," cries Cunliffe at once, with a bow, "to ride for Mistress Heron."

'"Ay," says t' Squire, "an' t' night before a message will doubtless come to say that Mr. Cunliffe has suddenly been called away

on important political business, an' he's much
grieved to forego a pleasure he had been so
much looking forward to."

' "You've said quite enough, sir," cries
Cunliffe, red an' passionate; "kindly have
your horse saddled—t' light-roan one for
choice; for I take your wager an' will ride
your horse home this night."

' T' Squire goes out to t' stable himself,
gives his orders, an' in fifteen minutes' time
t' horse is round at t' door.

' "Ye'll be wantin' a switch likely," says t'
Squire, as he shows him downstairs, "an' if
ye'll come into t' gun-room here, ye can take
your pick o' crops, or cuttin' whips, or what
ye will."

' T' room was dark, an' Cunliffe, he bumps
up against a small pail o' something an' upsets
it on his trousers and all over t' floor before
t' Squire gets a candle lighted.

' "Never mind, never mind that," says t
Squire cheerily, "it's just nowt to matter; it's
just for to try my hounds with to-morrow, an

shouldn't have been there. See, there's t' whip-stand ; take your choice," says he.

'Cunliffe, he takes a cuttin' whip, an' jumps on t' horse without more ado, an' goes out into t' paddock with t' stud groom, who is to show him where to start from when t' Squire shouts "off" from the roof of the house.

'A minute or two later t' Squire shows himself on t' battlements, and Mistress Heron's there too, to see the sport.

'"Are ye ready?" rings out t' Squire's voice.

'"Yes," comes back t' answer.

'"Then off!" he shouts down and drops t' handkerchief.

'Away he goes at a full gallop straight across t' wide-spreading west park-land, then draws rein a moment as he approaches t' haha with a drop of five feet or so, perhaps. Just as he pulls up there comes a faint "you-yowin'," as of hounds upon a scent, from around t' corner of t' house.

' " Whatever's that ?" cries Mistress Heron quickly, as she catches the sound of it.

' " Why, it's t' hounds," cries t' Squire, with a stabbing laugh. " I thowt it might help him t' jump t' black beck an' win his wager to have t' hounds after him, an' so it will, for there's a bit aniseed sprinkled on Gamecock's fetlock bandages, an' Cunliffe's stepped into some himself."

' " 'Tis the deed of a savage !" says my lady, and with a proud contempt of him she steps away from his side as far as t' battlements will permit.

' Away go t' hounds wi' riotous music hot upon t' scent ; on, forrard on they go, right over t' haha and up and across t' pasture beyond, at t' end of which, and beside t' beck, Cunliffe was galloping up an' down trying to find an easier place. It appears he hadn't, in his excitement, taken notice of t' hounds giving tongue, or looked behind him, but all of a sudden he perceives it, and halting his horse stockstill, looks behind him.

Then it seemed to flash upon him what's up, and he forces back t' horse some twenty yards or so—first hounds racing towards him about hundred yards behind—rams in t' spurs, cuts him with t' whip, and claps him at it. Game-cock tries it bravely, and leaping high into the air just lands on t' further bank, but short a bit, and on t' soft edge, and pecks forward badly on his head, sending Cunliffe somersaulting over like a shot rabbit.

'"T' bet's won!" shouts the Squire, marking t' horse pick himself up before his rider and gallop away by himself over t' far field; "t' damned cockney cannot ride at all."

'"Yes, you've won your bet," replies my lady, gathering her skirts together and hold-ing them close as she passes him by, "but possibly you may have lost remembrance that you were born a gentleman," and with that she proudly turns her back and sweeps away down t' stairs.

'Well, t' hounds couldn't get across t' beck, and t' Squire's first whip was ready

wi' t' horn to fetch them back again ; so
Cunliffe was safe enough, but sorely damaged
an' bruised, an' 'twas a full week before he
left his house, when straight he goes abroad
on foreign travel.

'Things gradually went on from bad to
worse twixt t' Squire and Mistress Heron
after that night's play ; she used to lament
for Lunnon an' its fashions, an' on t' last
night of all she set t'owd Squire's blood
blazin' by sneerin' at " country yokels " and
their drunken ways.

' "Why, damn t' —— !" cries he, quite
forgetting himself, and using a word more
suitable to t' kennels than t' drawing-room,
" ain't we been here since King Alfred?
An' what can ye want more than that ?"

'Swift as fire she answers him, " One
might wish that they were gentlemen," says
she, an' cold an' contemptuous she walks past
him out of the drawing-room and up into her
own room, where she orders her maid to
pack up for her at once, an' 'tis but an hour

later when she drives away in t' carriage an'
never sees t'owd place again.

'Well, they separate by law, an' shortly
after, when t' bairn comes to live with his
father, Mistress Heron gets much taken up
with one of those father parsons, famous as
a preacher in Lunnon at that time.

'Finally, she goes into a sort of retirement
and becomes head of a sisterhood shortly,
which gets to be very famous for its Good
Samaritan sort of deeds.

'Grandfather used to say that whatever
she took up she would be sworn to do better
than anybody else. "Fox-'untin' she learnt
clever in six months' time, an' if ye can larn
that ye can larn owt," says he

'As for t'owd Squire, he hunts harder
than ever he had done before; an' nowt,
positively nowt, can stop him across country,
nor liquor stagger him, so that many
thought he was heartier an' happier than
ever he had been before.

'His son, as he grew up, was a bit trouble

to him, certainly, as he was a wild lad—just like himself, but with a touch of his mother's pride, so that it was just as well when he went into t' army an' was sent to t' Indies.

' Well, time sped on, and t'owd Squire's hair was turnin' gray, when news came that his wife—Sister Eva, as they called her—had died suddenly in her retreat or convent.

' Up goes t' Squire to Lunnon without a word, an' when the chief mourners—all of them ladies of t' sisterhood, in their white dresses—were liftin' up t' coffin ropes to carry it to t' graveside, an' ancient gentleman, clad in a queer, long, bottle-green tail-coat, with a high stock and beaver hat on t' back of his head, comes forward an' quietly takes hold of t' head ropes.

' T' sisters remonstrate with him, and ask him who he is. " Mesdames," says he, " I was her unworthy husband," and he doffs his hat as he speaks, and without another word spoken helps to carry her to her grave.

''Twas said that they were t' same clothes he had worn on his wedding-day.

'It would be some months after this that my grandfather was dinin' with t'owd Squire, after t' opening meet of t' season.

'"Here's to fox-huntin'!" cries he, after t' cloth was removed; an' a bit later he rises solemnly in his chair, an' he says, "And here's to a saint in heaven!" an' as he drinks it down grandfather sees a tear tricklin' on his cheek.

'Little by little he tells him all about t' quarrel and what had completed it: "And she was right, by G—!" cries t' Squire at the end of it, "as she always was, though I was too proud to say so then; and now it's too late, for she's a saint in heaven."

'That was the only time he spoke of her; but for all that, grandfather said it was clear that he was just broken-hearted, was t' poor owd Squire, even though five minutes after he was challenging him to ride for a fiver when 'ounds should find on t' morrow's mornin'.

'T'owd Squire never went better in his life, they said, than he did that day ; but just at t' close of it his horse made a mistake over some timber, and he came a cropper in a ploughed field, with his horse on top of him, and had three of his ribs broken.

'It was a baddish fall ; but though the doctors pulled him through he never got the better of it, and was taken away before t' season was out ; and he was glad to go, was poor owd Squire, for he said he believed she had forgiven him, but he couldn't rest till he knew for certain.'

AN AMMYTOOR DETECTIVE

'TELL me about that mysterious affair of "Tom the Scholar," and Jack Jefferson's sudden death, and how you ran him to ground when suspicion had given up the chase. If all I have heard is true, you ought to have been at Bow Street, high up in the Criminal Investigation Department. Tell me,' I said again, 'how you came to play the part of amateur detective.'

'There was nowt o' the ammytoor aboot it,' retorted 'the Heckler' with aggressive dignity, 'it was a proper perfessional bit o' wark, an' the pollis was fine put oot that they hadn't had a hand in it. Wey, there was Scott, wor pollis; he came to us an' he says, "If ye had only tell 't me about it I could

hev made a job on 't," says he, "'stead o'
lettin' him gan an' commit a fellor, d' y' see?"

' "No," says I, "I divvn't see; it was him
that done it, an' it was us as copped him, an'
if I hadn't taken it intiv hand, wey, thoo
would have still been usin' long words an'
followin' up yor clue like an aad blind man
followin' efter his dog," says I, "for I've no
sort o' notion o' the pollis; they nivvor finds
out nowt for themselves, ye hev elwis ti tell
them what it is ye want done, an' then at the
finish gan an' do it yorsel'."

' No, no; the pollis is just what the lawyer
chaps call "accessories efter the fac'"—
meanin' they comes up ti ye when aal's ower
an' done wi', like the bairns at the school-
sports, each one expectin' a prize.

' Well, as I was sayin', I copped "Tom the
Scholar" aal maa lane, an' I doot whether
anyone else could hev done it but me. I
had suspected him a while back, for he was
a mistetched* chap, ye ken, one o' the sort

* ' Mistetched ' = spoiled; of ill habits. *Cf.* Chaucer's
' tetch,' a spot.

that has a bit grudge against everythin', an'
vicious same as horses is sometimes, unfor-
gettin', unforgivin'—just a nasty disagreeable
beggor, ye ken.

'He was a scholar, though—" Tom the
Scholar" they called him—an' was aye busy
wi' books, nivvor had his head oot o' them,
whether at the Institute or at aad Mistress
Swan's, where he lodged.

'Efter a bit he takes up wi' courtin' Mary
Straughan, her who got married on Jack
Jefferson, an' I b'lieve she had a mind for
him once, but not for long, for he frightened
her biv his strange ways, an' a passionate
way o' talk he had, an' she gave up walkin'
wiv him an' took up wi' Jack instead—a
south-country chap that had come frae Yorkshire—a big, burly, thick-headed sort o' chap,
but tarr'ble good-natured.

'Well, Tom, he takes it varry badly, an'
just before they gets "called" i' church he
tarrifies Mary wi' vague threats as ti what'll
happen if she dares ti wed wi' Jack. Noo,

6

Tom was a "spirritualist," ye ken, as weel as a scholar, an' he swears that the spirits forbade the match, an' would be properly savage if they was disobliged.

'She was a narvious sort, was Mary, an' she tell't Jack ov't, an' Jack, he says, iv his queer clipp't Yorkshire way o' talk, "T' spirrits be d——d!" says he; "an' if that softy Tom comes interferin' 'twixt thoo an' me, I'll make him softier than ever," he says, shakin' a great big hairy fist that looked like a bullock's head.

'Well, they gets theirsel's married wivoot askin' leave either o' the "spirrits" or o' Tom, an' as nowt happened, an' Jack forbye was tarr'ble lucky iv his cavils * just efter his marriage, even Mary began ti laugh at the idea o' Tom an' his "spirrits" an' aal.

* 'Cavil'=the quarterly ballot amongst coal-hewers for their places down the pit. Seams differ greatly in quality and depth of coal, and in ease of working. This is the miners' own rough-and-ready method of adjusting the inequalities.

'They was tarr'ble happy those two, an' I
mind well hoo proud and triumphant-like
Jack looked as he slapped us on the back
one early summer mornin' as we went ti the
pit on the fore-shift, for I was only a hewer
then, same as himsel', an' not what I is now
—checkweighman, an' half ov a magistrate
as well, bein' vice-chairman o' wor lokil
District Council*—an' he cries, " Geordie,"
he says, " Geordie, man, I's that happy I can
scarcely haud myself in.   There's nowt I
couldn't do.   I could hew as much in one
shift as any five men together in two; I
could lepp ower a hoos, I's that cobby.   I
could challenge wee Bob Aitchison, t'
sprinter, to a quarter-mile, an' lay t' fortnight's wages that I'd best him too.   I could
sing, I b'lieve," he says, an' wiv a solemn
voice on him he adds: " Ay, an' I could
even put up a bit prayer—though I's not
much ov a Churchman—almost as weel as

---

* The chairman of a local District Council is *ex-officio*
a magistrate.

t' priest himself. An' I'll tell thoo why.
It's because Mary tells me that there's likely
gawin' to be an addition to the fam'ly party
sometime shortly. She's a rare well-bred un,
too, is Mary, an' I'll lay it's twins." "I'll gie
ye the best o' luck," says I, "but twins is
tarr'ble expensive, for I've tried 'em," says I.
"Man alive!" cries he, holdin' up his arm
—a proper colossyum ov a limb—"look at
that. If that cannot win bread for a dozen
o' twins, then a lighted candle cannot fire
gas," says he.

'He was a fine brave man,' continued 'the
Heckler' slowly, 'an' I can see him still
standin' on the heapstead, an' I mind hoo
pleased he was that he could hear a lark
singin' high i' the air ower heid just as the
sun peeped up before we went doon i' the
cage that mornin' for the last time together
—just as full o' life an' vigour he was as thoo
is noo—but for all that it was the last time I
saw him alive i' this world.

'It was the vary next mornin' that he was

killed, but I wasn't doon the pit that day, for
I had happened a bit accident the day before
through a shot that went wrang on us, an' I
was laid up i' bed for a week wiv a bandage
ower my eyes. I bear the marks yet,' and
he pointed to some small blue punctures, not
unlike shot marks, that the gunpowder had
left round about his left eyelid and cheekbone.

'Aal I could hear was that he had been
knocked doon biv a runaway galloway pony
that a lad called Harry Nicholson used to
drive. Harry, ye must ken, was a bit weak
iv his intellectuals, hevin' been born iv an
ower great hurry like before his bit intellect
had had time ti ripen, through his mother's
gettin' a gliff at an accident that had happened
her man doon the pit.

'Well, Harry was a driver, as I said, an'
he an' the galloway was comin' doon an
incline wiv a full tub, an' the galloway, hevin'
bolted, dragged the tub off the lines, an' came
blindly tearin' along this side an' that smash
up inti Jack as he rounded an awkward

corner.   He was fearfu' knocked aboot when he was picked up, they said, his head bashed in bi the tub's wheels, an' there he lay, dead as mutton.

'The crowner comes doon an' sits on the body, an' the jury bring it in " Death by mis'dventure " slap off, bein' iv a hurry likelies ti get oot for their dinners, an' there the whole thing would have ended wiv a buryin' an' a gettin' up mevvies ov a bit subscription fer his missus an' the bairn ; ay, that's hoo it would have ended up had it not been for "the Heckler."

'I wasn't allowed oot by the doctor, sae I was just forced to think it oot aal maa lane —mevvies havin' my eyes blindfolded helped us a bit ; anyways, I lay there quiet i' bed an' found I could think it aal oot like Gladstone ; ay, an' I tell thoo that Gladstone an' Horbert Spencor together cudn't have thought harder than I did at that period o' time, nor have pieced the puzzle together bettor than us.   It sounds like a bit brag, mevvies, but it isn't, by Gox! it's just the naked truth.

'Well, there I lay between the sheets wi' my "linin's" on, detarmined that if there had been any foul play nowt but death should stop us frae findin' it oot. First thing I does is ti get the wife ti ask Harry Nicholson in ti tea wiv us, so as ti hear aal aboot hoo it happened.

'Well, efter he has been well filled oot wi' tea, an' spice loaf, an' jam an' aal, I gets him ti tell the whole story, an' then I axes him a few supernumerary questions.

'"Thoo'll ken 'Tom the scholar?'" I axes him—"him that's a stoneman doon the pit, an' gans in for spiritualism an' sich like for his hobby an' pastime?" "Ay," he says, "I ken him nicely. Wey, I been at some ov his 'seeantics,' or whativvor it is he calls them, an' I have the makin' ov a fine 'mee-jum,'" he says, "for I can parsonate folks ov aal kinds, males an' females, wivoot any distinction o' sexes."

'"Ay!" says I, interruptin' him wiv a sort ov admirin' surprise i' my tone o' voice, "can thoo, noo? Wey, thoo's a clivvor one, that's what thoo is."

'"Ay," says he, quite enlarged at the thought, "an' there's some folk says that I isn't quite right i' the head, but they couldn't parsonate Alexander the Great—him that the sword-dancers sing aboot—like as I can. Could they, noo?"

'"No," says I, "not they. They're not scholars enough for that, an' mevvies they would be gliffed at it as weel. Dis thoo nivvor get a gliff at the spirits?" I axes, careless like.

'"Not while I's parsonating, I divvn't, but whiles when I's doon the pit I gets a gliff," says he; "it's sae dark an' lonesome i' places."

'"Dis Tom ivvor try to make thoo parsonate doon i' the pit?" I axes him, "for Tom, bein' stoneman, 'll come across thoo at times drivin' yor galloway."

' "Ay, I've seen him doon below," he
says, "though he nivvor talked on aboot
parsonating, but usuallies passes us by
wivoot sayin' nowt, for Tom's a vary distant
sort o' chap, thoo knaas."

' "But sometimes mevvies he would speak
wi' thoo when he passed thoo, an' other folks
wasn't aboot? Did he ivvor talk on aboot
the spirits ti thoo at all? That day the
galloway ran away, did he speak wi' thoo
that mornin'? Mevvies he did, laddie, an'
mevvies he told thoo not ti speak aboot it
lest the spirits wouldn't like it, or some
such kind ov argument," says I, insinuatin'
it tiv him like one o' thae lawyer chaps iv
a wig.

' "Ay, he spoke tiv us that mornin', sure
enough, sayin' as hoo he thought the spirits
was vexed, for he had heard them callin' i'
the pit itself through the darkness, an' he
wanted ti knaa whether I had heard the
voices same as himself or not. Well, I
hadn't heard nowt, nor had nivvor thought

aboot spirits bein' doon the pit, but I gets a
bit gliffed myself at that, an' a bit later I
ackshally heard them speakin' aloud—sure
an' certain," says he.

'"Did they gliff thoo just before the
galloway ran away an' ran ower poor Jack
Jefferson?" says I.

'"Ay," says he, "I got a gliff then, for I
heard the spirits' voices shootin'* oot against
us."

'"Gox!" says I, "to think o' that, noo!
Wey, thoo gies us a gliff an' aal; an' what
dis thoo hear them sayin'?" axes I.

'"'Here's the parsonator,' they shoots
out aloud, 'that calls us frae wor rest. Lepp
oot upon him, an' torment him! At him,
Annexo!' or some such ootlandish name,
—'at him, spirits aal!'"

'"Sae thoo starts awa' likelies wi' the
galloway at a gallop, an' couldn't get him
stopped on the incline?" I axes him.

---

* 'Shootin'' (shouting). 'Shuttin',' on the other
hand, would mean shooting, whereby quaint confusions
have occasionally arisen.

' " No, no, I was ower flay'd mysel' ti do
owt ; but the galloway must have gotten a gliff
at something. I mind I thought I saw a flash
o' light just at the moment, an' the galloway
he couldn't abide a sudden light across his
eyes, he was that narvious ; or mevvies it
was the voice that gliffed him same as it did
us ; anyways, awa' aff he goes wivvoot me,
an' dashes aff doon the incline wiv us chasin'
him an' shootin', ' Woa, woo-h, Paddie ;
woo-ah, thoo daftie !' "

' " An' hoo far behind him dis thoo think
thoo was when he come to the corner where
he ran inti poor Jack ? Did thoo see Jack
theesel', or hear him shoot out as the
galloway butted him ?"

' " No," says he, " I nivvor seen him, an'
I wasn't far behind the galloway nowther,
for as soon as the tub got awa' frae the lines
he couldn't travel vary fast, for it was loaded.
Aal I could hear was the bumpity-bump o'
the tub, then smash inti the wall—smash—
smash—an' a crash as the tub swung ower

an' dragged the galloway wiv it. I can mind nae mair nor that, mistor," says he, at the end ov his tale, "for I fell slap ower Jack Jefferson's body i' the darkness, an' pitchin' full upon my head was knocked senseless, till they come along an' picked us up. An' that's the whole story, Mister Carnaby," says he, "an' I've done wi' the spirits, an 'parson- atin', an' aal noo, for they're treacherous things, there's nae doot aboot it," says he.

'Weel, that was aal I could get oot ov him, sae I gives him some sweeties an' lets him gan, biddin' him not let on that I'd axed him any questions, ye ken, an' efter that I lay i' bed thinkin' it aal ower an' makin' up a plan o' campaign for when "the Heckler" should be up an' aboot again.

'Efter aboot another three days I was allowed oot by the doctor wiv a sort o' lamp- shade ower my eyelids, an' the next day bein' "pay Saturday," an' the pit idle, I detarmines within my ain mind ti gan doon maa lane an' hev a look round by myself; for it's no use

trustin' anyone else when ye've got a job o'
that calibry iv hand, ye ken.

'I kenned where the trajiddy had taken
place, o' course, sae I detarmines ti gan ti
the spot an' make a sarious of obsarvations.
"First place," I says ti myself, "there winnot
be much change i' the surroundin's, for it's
a new drift in by there that they are drivin',
wi' 'Tom the Scholar' an' his marrow, an'
not many workin'; an', secondly, it's damp
there wi' the salt water oozin' in through the
rock, sae that footmarks will have a good
chance ti stand a bit."

'Noo, "Scholar Tom" had a tarr'ble large
footprint, ye ken, an' it was that I was i'
search o', for I had my suspicions o' what
might have happened, an' I was convinced
that that d——d, mistetched beggor was at
the bottom o' poor Jack Jefferson's sudden
endin'—ay, an' whenivvor I thought o' that
fine, brave chap an' his bright face an' his
happiness, I says ti myself, "There'll be no
rest nor pleasure nor nowt for 'the Heckler'

till the mystery's discovered ; an' it's yor job ti discover it," I says ti myself.

'He was bound ti have been there, for, o' course, it was him as shooted out that nonsense at Harry that had gliffed him, an' dootless it was him that had flashed his davy i' the galloway's eyes.

'Jack, d'ye see, would have been lousin' off frae his wark an' walkin' doon the drift at that time when the galloway started off ; but what beat me was that Jack couldn't hev got oot o' the way i' time, bein' fine an' active, grand at hearin' and seein', an' ne fool forbye that.

'Noo, just when I had detarmined upon this i' maa mind a sort ov an inspiration takes us aal ov a sudden. "Wey divvn't thoo take that driver lad alang wi' thoo ti show thoo exactly where the trajiddy happened?' it says tiv us just as thoo it was a real, genu-ine voice i' my inside. "Sink me!" thinks I, "it's a tarr'ble clivvor idea, an' sae I will."

' " Has thoo anything else ti add ti that, Inspiration ?" I axes it, an' shortlies efter it says, " Divvn't thoo trust ower much ti what Nicholson says, nor tell him o' yor plan beforehand, for he's i' Tom's power, an' tarrified ov him," it says again.

' " Gox !" thinks I, " but this is the champion ; wey, I's as good a spiritualist as Tom himself."

' " There's one last question I must ax thoo," says I, for I hadn't properly thought beforehand o' the difficulty o' gannin' doon the pit on " pay-Saturday," an' that is : " Hoo i' the warld can us gan in-bye ? for thoo kens that naebody but the furnace-man, engine-man, an' horse-keeper gans doon that day, an' if anyone else wanted ti, wey, he would have ti get leave frae the manager, an' even then he would have ti have a deputy alang wiv him. Answer us this, Inspiration," says I, " an' it's a clagger for thoo, I's warned."

' But, mevvies efter two minutes, it whispers back two words, " drift," an' " beer."

'" Drift?" I repeats, an' " beer ?" An'
then aal at onst I sees the implication, for
I kenned the lodge-keeper at the head o'
the drift nicelies, an', what's mair, I kenned
what Sammy Cuthbertson, the local preacher,
calls " the joint iv his harness " still better.

' Sae I gans up tiv him quietly, an' I says
tiv him, " Geordy," says I, " hoo much o'
the best beer will five bob procure iv an
emergency ?"

'" Five bob," says he, vary serious, " will
buy aal but two gallons o' the best bitter,
an' d—— the emergency," says he.

'" Dis thoo prefer it i' bottles, or iv a
greyhen, or iv a pail—an' aal at onst?" says I.

'" Bottles is no use," says he, ' wey, the
corks alone will mevvies take a pint ti theirselves. Na, na, gie it ti me iv a pail for aal-
roond drinkin'."

'" Well," says I, "thoo shall have it iv a
pail if thoo'll just let us an' the lad here gan
in doon by the drift for an hour ti investigate
a private matter o' wor ain—just a visit ov

inspection. No harm done, nobody need ken, an' up again within the hour, I'll promise thoo that," says I.

' Well, his face prolonged itself at that a bit. " But if it was kenned," says he, " I'd get my notice."

'" Nobody will ken but us three," says I ; " an', look thoo, thoo shall have the pail at yor dinner to-morrow forenoon," says I.

' That did the business for him, I's warn'd, an' he promises ti oot wiv his key an' let us gan in by. Poor chap, though, he got his notice aal the same, though it wasn't my blame : it was because he was ower-greedy an' thought he could get another pailful oot o' somebody else later.

' Well, I says nowt ti Nicholson aboot gannin' doon the pit till the vary mornin', and then I gans along an' catches ahaud on him, an' says, " Ho-way,* thoo mun come along wiv us doon the pit, for I wants ti see the place o' the accident myself, an' I hev

* Come along.

7

arranged aboot gannin' doon," I says. Well, he turns quite white at this, an' whines an' cries not ti gan ; but I was res'lute wiv him, an' tarr'fies him wiv a hint ov a gaol if he winnot come doon and show us aal I axes him.

'Well, we went by the drift and straight doon ti the " Number 3, North," or " Joan " district, as we call it worsels, an' there we gropes aboot the trolley-way, just at the corner where the accident must have taken place' an searched for footmarks.

'The lad, ye ken, must just have started frae the putter's flat wiv a full tub, an' aboot thirty yards doon he must have been gliffed. Hereaboots, iv a fenced place, Tom must have waited on Jack's "loosin' off" frae his wark, an' another ten yards further on is where the galloway must have run awa' off frae the rails. I had it aal mapped oot ready i' my mind, an' it was just the details I had ti fit in wiv it.

'There was mair tramplin' aboot than I had expected, what wi' the galloway's stumblin', the tub ploughin' alang through the dirt, an' the footprints o' the search-party that had come up ti the scene o' the casualty ; but for aal that, I could see here an' there the marks o' Tom's big shoes, wi' the extry broad plates at heel an' toes he used ti wear.

'Mevvies it wasn't ower much ti see, but it heartened us up, for it conformed us i' wor opinions, especially the fact that wherever they was visible they was close in by the wall-side, as if he had been wishful ti hide himself as far as might be—a sort o' presumptuous evidence against him, as the lawyers call it.

'" I will have ti gan back ti bed again," I says ti myself, "ti think it aal oot properly, for though I haven't a doot about it myself, I'll have ti convince aal thae thick-heads o' judges at my lord's 'Size* before I gets him properly convicted, sae I must have it aal pieced oot an' put together like a bairn's puzzle-map."

* The Assizes.

7—2

'Well, we was slowly makin' wor way oot o' the passage when I hears something comin' up-by, creak, creakin' as it came. Weel, I's no coward, I's warn'd, an I'll face any man livin' that ye like ti mention, but I got a fair gliff at that, for I couldn't make oot what it might mean—Nicholson an' us bein' the only folk aboot doon there. "Gox, it's Jack's ghost!" think I ti mysel iv a sudden sweat o' fear. Sae oot at once I turns my davy (lamp), an' the lad's, fearin' lest he might notice us, an' shrinks back inti the corner o' the wall as small as could be, with the lad tremblin' aal ower next us. Efter a bit I sees a wee glimmer o' light shakin' i' the darkness, then a shadow ov a man behind it, an' slowly, vary slowly, as if seekin' something, it mounts up the passage towards us.

'"Hist!" says I ti the lad iv a thick whisper, "just smear your face an' hands ower wi' clarts, or the ghaist will cop us," I says, an' grabbin' a handful I clarts his face

an' hands iv an instant o' time; then I
scrapes up a handful for mysel' an' aal, but i'
reachin' oot for a good fill o' clarts my
hands struck up against a sort ov a heavy
bar o' some specie or other.

'I gied a bit haul at it, an' awa it comes
up inti my hands—a small, heavy, but handy
bit ov iron it was, mevvies about sixteen
inches long, wiv a sort o' knob at the end o't.

'"I'll have a look at thoo later," says I,
an' claps it inti my pocket wi' the one hand,
whiles I clarts my face wi' the other.   Mean-
time the creakin' thing was drawin' nigher
an' nigher tiv us, but the light wiv it was
tarr'ble dim, an' I couldn't have given it a
name.

'On came the light an' the shadow, but
the creakin' noise had stopped ; 'stead o' that
there was a squelch, squelch, as ov a man
steppin' in an' oot' o' mud.

'It passed us biv a finger's breadth, an' I
almost shouted aloud by way o' relief, for it
was a real live flesh-an'-blood man, wiv a

fouled davy, an' no ghost—for ghosts canna spit, I's warn'd.

'" D—— thoo !" I was just aboot ti shoot at him, comin' flayin' folk i' that fashion. " Who is thoo, thoo——" when he stops short on a sudden, just round the corner above us, an' talks tiv himself oot loud. " Ay, it'll be just aboot here," he muttered, " that it fell," and I could have let flee a yell o' delight that would have brought a fall o' stone doon, for it was no other voice than " Tom the Scholar's " himsel'.

'" Thoo b——!" I says ti mysel', an' clenches my fist tight ; " thoo b——! but I's copped thoo noo."

'" Tell ti me noo, Annexo," continues Tom, usin' the same furrin' sort o' talk as he had ti the lad ; " tell ti me noo where it lies —the weapon that freed my destined bride frae unlawful arms. I mun hev it back, for there's a d——d chap i' wor village that they call 'the Heckler,'" he gans on, the impittent scoondrel that he was, " a daft feller

that's mad aboot dogs an' sic' like nonsense,
but he has his suspicions, an' mevvies might
be dangerous, for he has been questionin'
my meejum, Nicholson, the driver lad.'
Speak then, Annexo, speak, my beauty.
Where lies my trusty weapon? Speak
louder," says he again, impatient like, "for I
canna hear i' the darkness."

'Just on that instant I gets another
inspiration i' my insides, an' wivvoot mair
ado I whispers oot loud iv a fine, feminine,
and superfluous voice: "Search ti the right
hand a bit lower doon, canny man," says I,
"an' thoo'll find what thoo is wantin'," an' I
held oot my hand ready ti grasp his wi' when
he stretched it oot.

'"Aha!" says he, quite gratified like, "sae
thoo has found a voice, has thoo?"

'It was nigh pitch darkness about us, for
his davy had almost gane clean oot wi' the
clogged wick, but I could feel his hands
gropin' towards us, an' I says ti mysel',
"Another foot, an' a murderer's copped!"

'His hands came hoverin' ower mine, for I could feel the wind o' them; in another second he touches us, an', grabbin' ahaud ov him by way o' reply, I shouts oot, "Ay, here's Annex-us, thoo b—— !"

'The yell he let oot was fearfu', an', startin' back, he dragged his arm oot o' my grasp, an' then leaped forward iv a flash, ducked past us, an' awa off round the corner he fled, us efter him like the aad bitch* efter a started hare.

'He had dropped his lamp, an' it was darker nor Hell itself, but I could hear him dashin' along i' front ov us at wondrous speed.   Mad keen I was, as I tore efter him ower bits o' balk an' stone lyin' aboot doon the rolley-way, bended double sae as ti avoid the roof-beams.   Bang up against a door I comes, shakin' mysel' intiv a jelly by the shock, but when I had it opened an' was through I could still catch the sound ov his

* Viz., Bonnie Bella, a famous greyhound of 'the Heckler's.'

footfalls not far in front ov us. "He'll have come a big bat hissel' against the door," I thinks ti mysel' as I started off again, "ay, an' bein' before us he'll have aal the obstacles ti contend wi' first ov aal. Huzza, ho-way!" an' I tore efter him, a fair deevil for reckless-ness—makin' no doot he was for the main rolleyway, an' sae oot by the main drift by which we had entered the pit.

'There came the thud ov another door, an' I gans a bit mair cautious like, fendin' wi' my hands i' front ov us. Shortlies efter I notices that the footfalls sounded fainter-like; they seemed ti be comin' frae the left-hand side noo an' not i' front ov us.

'Aal ov a sudden I minds mysel' ov a return air-way that would lead oot by the main drift. "Gox!" I thinks, "thoo's hit the mark, but where the openin' is I cannot mind, for it isn't travelled biv any one barrin' the deputies. He passed the door i' front ov us, but bi the sound he's ti the left hand ov us noo;" sae I felt along the wall till I comes tiv an open way. "Ho-way," says I, mad ti think he might escape us efter aal, "ho-way, thoo'll get him yet!"

'On, on I went at a reckless speed, ti make up for my bad turn, an' iv another minute I gied tongue like a foxhound, for I heard him pat, pattin' on i' front ov us. "I's copped thoo!" I yelled through the darkness tiv him, ti tarr'fy him, for I heard him stumblin' amangst some loose props or gear o' some sort quite plainly, "I's copped the murderer!"

'Foot upon foot I gains on him; I hears him pantin' just a yard or two i' front ov us. I grasps oot wi' my hands an' touches his shoulder, an' he yells wi' terror, givin' a leap like a hare, an' slips frae under my hands.

'Doon, full length, doon I fell wiv a smash like a fall o' stone, half stunned, my head like a night o' stars.

'Suddenly there comes a yell o' horror— then a thud, a clump, clump, an' a c-clush,

an' then stark silence, an' doon, right doon
at the bottom ov a staple fifteen fathoms
deep ten yards i' front ov us lay aal that
was left o' the murderer copped, clean copped,
by "the Heckler." '

' AY, that's what 'tis,' replied 'the Heckler'
to my query, 'it's an "in memoriov'm"
—Latin, ye ken, meanin' in memory ov him.
The words is alike, mevvies, but it's Latin
language, I's warn'd, an' I howked it oot
upon that headstone myself wiv a clasp-
knife.'

I knelt down upon the sandy dune and
brushed aside the bents that nearly covered
the squat gray stone with their long lashes,
and eventually deciphered a straggling array
of figures which for their illegibility would
have enraptured an antiquary.

'It was just below us,' continued 'the
Heckler,' 'that I found his cap, an' thinkin'
him drooned, an' him bein' a favour·yte wi'

me, I just put up that bit stone for him an'
carved his initials on it, an' the Latin, an'
G. C., that's for us, "the Heckler," ye ken,
his mark. But it was a false alarm efter aal,
an' noo that Jim Hedley's a Right Hon.
Lord Mayor oot iv Australie, I's warn'd but
when he's put under the sod he'll hev a
hearse an' four horses an' a proper musulyum'
(mausoleum) 'tiv hisself.'

'What made you think he was drowned?'
I inquired. 'Did you think it a case of
suicide?'

'Ay, o' course I did; we aal did that,
an' not wivvoot reasons,' responded 'the
Heckler,' 'for he was full o' misery at that
time, an' wanted ti get shot o' the whole lot
ov it. Jim was a fine, tall, proper lad—
"bonny Jim" the lasses called him—wunnerfu' handy, too, iv aal sorts of ways, an' as
for behaviour, wey, he could talk ti my lord
as canny as tiv a pot-boy.

'Well, wiv aal these gifts o' fortune it
wasn't surprisin' he got hisself sweetheartin'

wiv a young, bonny, quiet-faced lassie, daughter ov aad Sheepshanks, the farmer, close in by the village.

'It was a bit lift for Jim, for she had some brass, but aad Sheepshanks, he tries to forbid the "callins"' (banns) 'i' church ; "for what's a pitman," says he, "that a farmer's daughter should marry on ?—a dirty-faced, drunken, dog-lovin', gamblin' chep," says he ; an' a lot o' gob o' that kind, ye ken, bein' a red-hot Tory wiv a lot o' Noah's-ark kind ov ideas iv his head.

'The lassie didn't think that, though ; she just warshipped Jim, followin' him aboot wiv her eyes everywhere, just like the aad bitch' (here he nodded towards the greyhound beside him) 'does "the Heckler."

'Well, they marries an' has a bit fam'ly, an' Jim gans ahead quick ; he was marrow' (mate) 'wi' me as a hewer yence, an' then he becomes a deputy, an' bein' a great reader an' a gran' speaker, there was some talk o' makin' him wor Member o' Parlyment when

he got a bit older. Well, it had aal been
plain sailin' for Jim so far, an' everybody
thought his success was sartin, but he soon
came tarr'ble nigh makin' a tragedy ov hisself,
poor chap.

'There was a young widow woman came
ti live doon here at the Prospect House
ower there. She'd been married on a fat
old chap that had made a lot o' brass i' the
toon i' publics, an' they used to come here
for a bit i' the summer, an' when he died she
comes doon ti the "Prospect" ti bide for
good an' aal.

'I sometimes think,' continued my companion after a slight pause, 'that it's a sair
pity folks isn't sometimes drooned like kittens
or "put under" same as dogs that turn oot
no use. It wud save a lot o' misfortunes an'
misery, I's warn'd, an' unless ye drooned a
Gladstone, or a John Wesley, or mevvies
even a "Heckler," the world would be aal
the better o't.

'Anyways, she should have been drooned

slap off as a babby, for she was a rank bad un—just rank bad ti the bone—an' when a woman is bad, she's just the devil's own viewer* or deputy, by Gox !

'She had been on the stage, 'twas said, at one time, an' there was queer stories aboot her, so that the gentry-folk aboot here would have nowt ti do wiv her, sae she had aal the better opportunity ti play her tricks wi' Jim.

'She was free wi' the brass, ye ken, an' give subscriptions awa for the askin', providin' she had her name an' address clagged up large on the play-bills, an' was a champion at gettin' up concerts for wor Mechanic Institute an' such-like entertainments.

'That was hoo she first got a hand upon Jim, for he had a gran' voice—a perfect champion at harmony he was, an' she just buttered him up properly. It was "Oh, Mr. Hedley, an' what a fortin ye would have made in the Opera!" "Sing it again, Mr. Hedley, it's fair ravishin'," an' so she carried

* Manager.

on till she had him awa to practise duetties wiv her at her hoos, an' made him stay ti supper wi' glasses o' wine tiv it—yellow shampain wine that'll set your brain iv a froth, I b'lieve, an' at the finish she has him just drugged wiv her enchantments.

'There was one night I mind I was oot walkin' an chanst ti pass by alang that road there that leads past the hoos—the trees wasn't grown up then, ye ken, an' I could spy a bit in through the windie, which was open on the night—it bein' summer then, d'ye see.

'She was settin' beside the pianner playin' pretence wiv it, an' castin' up white eye-glances at Jim soft-like, noo an' again, with a sort ov insolence, too, as though she kenned her power ower him—drawin' oot the very marrow an' soul ov him wiv her perfections.

'She was aal clad i' silks an' satins, like a play-actress—her bosom gleamin' wi' jools, an' Jim was leanin' against the pianner gazin' at her, fair drunk wiv her blandishments.

'I cuddn't stand by an' just do nowt ava, sae I let fly a yell upon the night, "Ho-way home ti thy own lawfu' missus, an' leave that d——d hussy alone."

'He gave a sudden start at that, an' leaps round ti the windie, claps it ti wiv a smash, an' pulls the curtains ower it.

'Well, I kenned then by that token that it was aal ower wi' Jim. She had him fast, an' nowt could be done, for interferin' i' them cases is warse than useless; but I was sair, sair grieved for him an' his wee quiet bonny-faced wife, an' I walked awa home callin' that woman aal things I could lay my tongue ti under heaven.

'Things went gradually from warse ti warse; he neglected his work an' avoided his wife, an' he became tarr'ble violent iv his temper, an' nigh offered ti fight me yence when I tried ti argy wiv him upon his foolishness. Well, the crissis comes one night when his wife follows him ti the Prospect Hoos an' walks straight inti the

drorin'-room where him an' the other woman
was. He'd just been threatened by the
viewer, d'ye see, wi' gettin' his notice if he
didn't pull hisself tegither, an' knawin' things
were aaltegither wrang wiv him, he just gans
slap off ti the woman oot o' pure recklessness,
for he was none o' yo'r half an' half gentlemen, an' as he was gannin' ti the deevil, wey,
he wud gan wiv a brass band, ye ken.

' His wife comes in upon them like a ghost,
an' never heedin' the other woman, cries tiv
him, haudin' oot her arms for him, "Oh,
come back, Jim, come back ; divvn't break
my heart !"

' Jim says nowt, but glares moodily on the
ground, an' there's silence for a bit. Then
the woman begins ti laugh saftly tiv herself,
eyein' Jim's missus scornfu' like frae top ti
toe standin' there, small an' shabby-dressed
an' tearfu', an', "Wey doesn't thoo gan ?"
says she, "here's yo'r hooskeeper come ti
fetch thoo home !" she says.

' Jim gies a start at this an' looks up wi'

blazing eyes at his temptress, then he says tiv his wife, "Gan home, Mary, gan home; this is no a fit place for thoo," an' sae she gans awa softly, weepin' like a desolate bairn.

'Soon as the door shuts he turns upon the other woman, an' he says sternly, "This is the end o't, Susan; I'm gannin' awa' an' ye'll never see me mair. You've plenty brass, an' can fend for yo'rself. I've given thoo my life, an' I can do nae mair; sae good-bye, my lass, for ever an' aye."

'But she rushes tiv him, an' clasps her arms roond aboot his neck an' sweethearts him an' swears they must get married; but Jim, he puts her quietly awa', an' wiv a stone-set face gans oot o' the hoos an' straight for the shore.

'Tossin' his cap on ti the ground, he walks right inti the waters an' begins swimmin' oot, right oot inti the sea, there ti droon hissel' an' his troubles straight awa.

'Well, mevvies he was ower strong ti be easy ti droon; mevvies the cold water cleared

his mind a bit, an' he thought shame on
hissel' ti leave wife an' bairns ti shift for
theirsels ; anyhoo, as he said efter, when he
saw the red light of a little schooner ridin'
waitin' for the tide off the harbour, a thought
cam intiv his brain, "Wey not gan right
awa an' make a fresh start iv a fresh place ?"

'The thought grows on him, an' he swims
oot ti the schooner just as she was standin'
awa for London town, an' he hails her an' is
taken on board i' the nick o' time. Another
minute an' she would have been oot o' sight
an' hearin', an' Jim would have been a corpse
in another ten minutes, I's warn'd.

'Well, nowt is heard ov him for months
an' months. "The Heckler" carves an "In
memoriov'm" on that headstone; his missus
gans inti "blacks," an' the other woman
leaves the Prospect Hoos an' gans right awa
from these parts.

'One day though, Jim's missus comes
alang tiv us cryin' an' laughin' aal at yence,
haudin' up a letter and kissin' it between

whiles. "It's from Jim! Jim!" she cries, "an' Jim, sweet Jim, he kept hissel' alive for me an' Jackie an' Sal! Oh, he loves me yet, my Jim!"

'Well, it seems as hoo he had gan oot tiv Australia, an' efter a bit wanderin' had gettened hisself a very canny sitivation at a gold mine, an' he sends aff at yence for his missus an' bairns, an' a week later awa they starts.

'They finds Jim doin' first-class when they gets there, an' he went ahead like a hoos-o'-fire as soon as he gets his missus an' bairns back tiv hissel', an' the past wiv its clartiness was just clean wiped out between them.

'An' noo he's the Right Honourable the Lord Mayor o' Ballarat, or some such place, an' cannot mak' enough ov his missus and bairns, they say.

'There's some women mevvies,' added 'the Heckler' in conclusion, 'who wouldn't have pardoned their man, but she was one o' the sort that are just faithfu' ti death—nowt can tarr'fy them aff, an' it's fair providential that it should be so, for there's many men noo livin' who wud just have been iv hell lang syne else.'

'THE HECKLER' UPON WOMEN-FOLK

'MEN are kittle cattle enough,' replied 'the Heckler' oracularly, from his position of vantage on the top of a gate, to some question of mine concerning an indignation meeting held recently to protest against some matter about which no two people could give a like account; 'but they're nowt ti what womenfolk is. Ye can get roond most men easy enough if ye've a bit tax.'

'Tax?' I queried aloud, somewhat mystified. What tax? not rates an' tax ——'

'Gan on wi' thoo—rates an' taxes be d——!' retorted the oracle swiftly. 'No, nowt ti do wi' them things; just tax, or tacts,

mevvies it is, meanin' a pleasant way wi'
ye, a bit touch o' the cap when the manager's
vext wi' ye, a turn o' management when a
drunken man wants ti fight ye for nowt at
aal, ye ken, an' sae forth. Wow, but ye can
fettle most things amangst men wiv a little
o' that social lubricant, but wi' women it's
different aaltigether ; tax is nae use wi' them ;
it's just throwin' pearls before swine.'

'Holloa !' I interrupted again. 'What
would the missus say to that ?'

'Not hevin' heard it, she'll say nowt,'
retorted 'the Heckler' severely.

'Well, as I was aboot to say when thoo
forgot theeself, and disturbed the meetin' wi'
yor interruptions, most men has foibles—
some's dog-men like myself, some's book-
men, some's gard'ners, some's beer-barrils,
an' sae forth, an' if ye mind this ye can get
what ye want usuallies oot o' them. But
women's a different breed aaltigether. They
divvn't care for the same things as men, an'
ye cannet get roond them, I's warn'd, for

they elwis gets roond ye instead. A man
has no ambitions till he's married, Maistor
John. Mevvies he's keen aboot this, an'
that, an' 'tother thing, but that's nowt. Noo,
woman's just chockfull ov ambitions aal her
life long, an's nivvor, no, nivvor, satisfied
from her cradle tiv her grave, an' even then
she's wantin' fower horses tiv her hearse.
Tak' a wee girlie for an instance: she's elwis
wantin' new claes; then she's wantin' a
man, then bairns, then a hoos ov her own,
then a better cloak than Mariarann nex'
door; an' when she gets them aal she's not
satisfied, not one little bit, but's warse than
ivvor.

'Noo I'll gie ye an instance o't.

'Ye'll dootless mind havin' seen or heard
tell ov Tom Archbold, yence fore overman
here i' the aad pit, a great, big, buirdly man,
champion hewer o' the colliery at one time,
who aye took the lead i' the village at every
bit sport, an' carry-on, an' jollification that
might be gannin' on at any time.

'Well, there was a little wee bit lassie ov aboot twenty-five years ov age, who had been married yence, but had lost her man iv an accident doon the pit—a fall o' stone, ye ken—an' nae sooner has she buried him than she's on the look-oot for anither mate.

'Well, bein' the littlest woman i' the village, she natorally—such bein' woman's human nature—tak's a fancy for the biggest man iv it, meanin' Tom Archbold, an' she gans for him straight awa.

'Ye'll hev seen a setter dog workin' for a partridge or a rabbit iv a rough grass field, mevvies. Weel, it was just the same method o' procedure wiv her. She gets a scent o' what she was wantin'; she draws upon him up wind; then she gets a tip-toe, steals tiv him till her breath's fair upon him, an' the man's done—fair done—clean copped, and it's " for better an' warse till death do us part."

'So it was wi' Lizzie an' Tom.

'Tom was a weeda (widower), an' on the

look-out for anither missus, an' havin' had a great big woman for his first—a proper marrow ov himself i' size an' shape—an' not havin' been ower well satisfied wiv his venture, he thinks he'll try a smaller article for his second lott'ry.

'Well, Tom was elwis very free an' open wiv his conversation, an' mevvies Lizzie, she gets ti hear ov it; but she pretends ti tak' no notice o' Tom when she passes along the Raa,* or meets Tom i' the street. She just sails past him, noo wiv head i' the air, again wiv her eyes upon the ground, mournfu' like for the loss of her man, an' Tom becomes quite bewitched by her manners, for she was a fair contrast wiv Bella, who had ti tarrify him wiv a summons from the pollis at the finish before she could get him ti marry her i' chorch.

'Well, she bags him clivvor at the finish, an' they gets theyselves married wivoot more ado.

* Row.

'A week efter comes "pay-Friday,"* an',
naturally, quite apart from the "celebration
of his nuptials," as the newspaper cheps say,
he gets hissel as boosy as can be, what wi'
standin' treat, an' bein' treat an' aal, an' efter
closin' time it was wi' some difficulty that me
an' my marrer gets him along home.

'We knocks on the door, an' we assists
him in, an' he staggers up tiv his missus, who
was sittin' iv her armchair knittin', an' tries
ti gie her a bit chuck under the chin. " Ho-
—way——," he stutters, " Lizzie, maa lass,
an' put us ti bed!" an stoopin' down iv a
staggerin' way ti kiss her loses his balance,
an' flops doon unexpected on the floor.
" Ye needn't wait," Lizzie says tiv us,
haughty-like, takin' no notice o' Tom, an'
sae oot we gans, an' leaves them. But we
just stops a minute ootside ti hear Lizzie gie
him his gruel ; an', wow ! but she let him

* Pitmen are paid fortnightly on the Friday : the following day is ' pay-Saturday.' Non-pay-Saturday is known
as ' baff-Saturday,' the derivation of which no man knows
to this day.

have it, an' no mistake! "Thoo great flamin' drunken lubbert!" says she, "comin' home ti my hoos at this time o' night, drunk as a lord, an' only been married a week!" she cries. "Thoo mun just get used wiv it, maa lass," says he solemnly from the floor; "for aa elwis gets drunk reg'lor on a pay-Friday; an' it'sh maa hoos thoo ——, for aa's maistor," he says, thinkin', mevvies, he mun assert hissel' even if he has had his gills.

'"Put thoo ti bed?" cries she. "Wey, I'll not touch thoo, nor let thoo touch me nowther till thoo's sober again, an's begged maa pardon."

'"Pardon-sh?" says Tom, an' laughs, fair amused by her impittence. "Wey, if maa legs wesn't sae wambly the night, I'd larn thoo a lesson, thoo ——"

'"Get up, an' try, thoo sponge o' beer," she says, an' snaps her fingers iv his face. "Get up, an' try," cries she again. "I daur thoo ti;" an' she actually has the impittence ti stir him wiv her foot. Just fancy that!

A yard an' a half o' petticoat, fair insultin'
upon a proper mountain ov a man like Tom !
The door was a bit open, d'ye see, an' my
marrer an' me could see them two comics
quite plain.

'Well, Tom, he thinks things is comin'
tiv a pretty pass if his missis is gannin' ti
clean her boots on him efter a week's
marryin'; so, much against his will, he pulls
hissel' tegither, an' by the help o' the bedpost
gets on his feet.

'"Wey," cries Lizzie again, lookin' him
ower mair scornfu' than ever, "thoo's as
unsteady on thy feet as a horse wi' the
staggers!" she says. "I could knock thoo
doon wi' one finger !"

'"I bet-sh a sovereign thoo cannet; ay,
an' anither that I'll drive yo'r lugs reet intiv
yo'r heid wi' one bat o' my fist," says he ;
an' he puffs hissel' oot as he searches for the
coin, an' spits on his hands iv a preliminary
sort o' way.

'Then, sudden, she comes up tiv him, gies

him a tap wiv her forefinger, unexpected like, straight on the breast, an' Tom, taken un- awares, lurches backward, catches his foot iv a bracket, crashes intiv a chair, an' falls wiv a tarr'ble thump an' a racket of furniture straight on ti the flaggin'. He gies a little lift ov his head as he looks up in a dazed way for a moment from the floor. Then he says, sinkin' back again, "There's been a fall o' stone; gan an' fetch the depity," he says, then sort o' dwams (swoons) awa.

'Lizzie, she looks him ower for awhile, cool as a policeman wiv a lantern, then lifts a pillow off the bed, an' puts it under his head as he lies stretched upon the floor. Next, she takes the boots off her man, an' sae leaves him ti bide where he lies, whilst she gans ti bed her lane.

'Next mornin' Tom feels hissel' as sick as a bad bat o' the head an' a wambly stomach can make a man, an' "lies in" while his missus gies him warm things ti drink, an' tends him like a bairn.

9

'Well, she has him properly caught, for he
has ti lie there idle the best part ov a week,
an' cannet work for another week efter that,
the skelp he'd got frae the fall bein' a serious
affair, as it seemed.

'When he gets up again he was sae savage
at the chaff he gets aboot bein' knocked
doon biv his missus that he gans back tiv
his hoos iv a hurry, tak's off his belt, an' is
gannin' ti strap her within an inch ov her life,
when she says, " Tom, an' who was it that's
been nursin' thoo this last fortnight ?"   An'
she axes it quietly, facin' him wivoot a
tremor, her eyes fixed upon his.

'Tom stands there wiv his arm uplifted ;
but though he was hot ti strike her, somehoo
or ither, as he said efter, he was fair bested
if he could manage it.

'Well, that was aboot the beginnin' an'
the end o't, for she'd conquered him properly,
an' Mister Six-Foot-Two soon found oot
he'd got a proper taskmaster for his missus,
even though she was but a yard an' a half

high, an' looked as though ye could have snapt her across yor arm. She didn't knock him doon again, but she was elwis surprisin' him inti startin things, an' when he tired ov it she would scorn him a bit, an' ask, "An' what's the good o' bein' a strong man if ye cannet show yor strength? Any fool can get drunk," says she, "an' lose his brass bettin'; but thoo's a strong man, Tom, I's warn'd, an' I've bet Ned Lee's wife a dollar that thoo can walk past the Pitman's Arms on pay-Friday night wivvoot ever lookin' inside!"

'Well, that was the way o't i' Lizzie's case. She soon had her Samson's locks clipped short, an' iv a few years' time he becomes a depity, a back overman, an' finally fore overman, has a hoos ov his own, an' a whole raa (row) o' cottages.

'Some has different ways from others,' reflected my companion, further, 'but aal womenfolk's ambitious.'

'Noo, tak' my own case—"the Heckler's"

9—2

—when I got married on the aad lady there was no nonsense aboot the business. " Ho-way," I says, " will ye tak' us, Betty ?" for I kenned nicely beforehand she was the right sort for us, havin' obsarved her previous, an' walked oot wiv her a Sunday night or two. "Ay, an' I will, Geordie," she says thankfully, an' as meek as skim milk ; but for aal that I've been got the best o' lots o' time biv her ambition, an' noo, here I is, wiv a fam'ly o' seven, an' the missus insistin' upon Harry's—that's the eldest boy, ye ken—gannin' ti the Grammar School ti parfect hissel' as a scholar. Ay, wor Harry's a proper scholar, I's warn'd, but schoolin's tarr'ble expensive.

'An' noo, I'll just gie ye this bit advice, Maistor John. Divvn't thoo get married unless thoo marries a heiress, for, I tell thoo, aal women's ambitious, an' ambition's a tarr'ble expensive hobby.

' Gox ! yes, just fearful, Maistor John.'

THE 'CALEB JAY'

(THE 'QUEL OBJÊT')

I.

THE 'Caleb Jay'* was not, as his nick-name of itself might testify, popula in our pit village of Black Winning. His appearance was against him in the first instance, and he continued to be shy and reserved even after you might be said to

* It is said that at the time of the Napoleonic wars some French prisoners were detained in custody in the pit country not far from Durham City. It would appear that some intercourse between the inhabitants of the place and the foreigners sprang up, which resulted in the addition of one expressive phrase, at least, to the local dialect, that, namely, of 'Caleb Jay' for 'Quel objêt!' due to their strange garb, probably, or tattered appearance. The phrase is now wholly obsolete, the writer believes, but it is said it was once actually in use.

have made his acquaintance. Reserve is unpopular in any society, but in the lower social grades, where life is of a freer and more hearty character than in the propriety-loving circles of the well-to-do, it may be said to be one of the 'seven deadly sins.'

There was no reserve about Tom, his elder brother, who was a good-looking, idle, somewhat dissolute youth of twenty-three years of age.

Tom was always ready to 'stand in' for a 'ha'penny loo,' never flinched from a 'bout at the beer,' could throw a quoit well, when his eye was clear and his hand steady, and was never at a loss with the lasses.

Tom, therefore, was a general favourite, being 'well ta'en up wi'' by all save a few of the more serious-minded people; and 'Caleb Jay' suffered, I think, partly through contrast with his brother.

'Caleb Jay' had been injured when working as a putter down the pit, and consequently was 'game of one leg.' He wore the cast-off finery of his brother, the coloured scarves and embroidered waistcoats of his festive occasions—out of economy, no doubt, but some said ' oot o' foolishness.'

Certainly they did not suit well with his sallow complexion and thin, peaked countenance, and with the big and weary eyes.

He worked now at any odd job he could find. He had the care of the viewer's strip of kitchen garden, and went round with papers, etc. ; but it was not much that he earned, apparently, for his mother, who doted on her handsome son Tom, was often heard to complain that he wasn't worth his keep.

He had a strange way of mysteriously disappearing for some days on occasion, sometimes even for a week at a stretch, and sundry persons, annoyed perhaps by his reticence, hinted at secret dissipation.

If closely questioned, he would admit having had a 'job i' the toon,' or 'ower away yonder,' pointing vaguely this way or that ; and gossip

had at least this confirmation for its un-
charitable suspicion, that he always returned
pale, tired and haggard-looking.

Some of the boys had tried to 'nab' him
either coming or going on one of these
expeditions of his, but he was 'cuter nor a
cushat,'* as I overheard a sporting youth
lament who had followed him in early morning all the way to Oldcastle, and there in the
suburbs had suddenly lost him just on the
brink of discovering the secret.

Gradually we became accustomed to his
flittings, and he was spied upon no more;
but for my own part I thought I had, by a
comparison of the times and seasons of his
absences, at least discovered this much—
that he was usually away at the incidence
of fairs and festivals.

I think I knew him more intimately than
any other person in the village, except,
perhaps, our Methodist minister, who never
rested till he had succoured any who might

* Wood-pigeon.

be in 'sickness, sorrow, or distress'; but to neither of us, I found, on comparing notes, had he ever vouchsafed any confidences.

The only way in which I eventually discovered I could be of any use to him was by lending him books. He was extremely fond of reading, and had a special taste for dramatic poetry, which he occasionally gratified by coming to my lodgings, and there devouring the historical plays and tragedies of Shakespeare.

I had once or twice on these occasions endeavoured to extort from him the secret of his absences, but the only result had been an increased reserve on his part, followed by an almost immediate departure from my presence, so that I had soon desisted from further questioning him on the point.

At the same time, I confess I entertained a lingering hope that I might one day be able to penetrate the mystery ; for mystery of some sort I was convinced it was, though not of a vulgar kind.

II.

It so chanced that I was detained in Bridgeton on the day of the annual fair and hiring, and having two hours to wait for my train, I determined to pass the time away by noting the humours of the festival. Farmers' wives, laden with 'remnants' and cheap bargains in the hardware line, were slowly surging through the throng, towards the various publics, in search of their 'men' and the 'trap.' Hinds, male and female, having now 'bound their bargains' with their masters, were coasting round the booths and stalls, 'putting in' at all the ale-houses they passed in their uncertain voyaging.

The men were somewhat sheepish still, not having taken sufficient beer on board as yet to lose the shyness of the countryman in town. They confined themselves to chaffing one another, to casting stray glances at their sweethearts, who tittered in their wake, and

to offering, when moved to gallantry, 'anuther
glass o' yel.'

A squad of pitmen here and there, their
customary rivalries heated with liquor, were
challenging each other noisily at the various
'try-your-strengths' and 'prove-your-powers'
that were anchored in the corners of the
market-place.

My attention was next attracted by the
clash of cymbals and flamboyant drum-
drubbings. ''Ere y'are, ladies and gents,
'ere y'are! Yo'r friend an' acquaintance Bob
Stevens, wiv his high-class dancin', trapezin',
Shakespearian an' variety entertainment!'

The great flaring gas-brackets, with their
smoky tongues stabbing the darkness fitfully,
lit up a most delectable advertisement. I
produced 'tuppence,' 'walked up,' as invited,
to the tent, and found myself in the 'hall of
amusement and instruction combined.' It
was already crowded, but I eventually discovered a seat in the far corner.

Cries of ' Back! back!'* were still ringing

* The Northumbrian for 'encore.'

in the air, and after a moment or two a most cadaverous - looking clown reappeared and advanced to the footlights.

His haggard, melancholy mien was in admirable artistic contrast to his garb and the burlesque humour of his song. '*And oh*,' sang he, at the end of each verse relating some contretemps of the bashful lover, '*it makes me very, very lively! Very, very lively!*' he repeated, as he step-danced up and down the tiny stage amidst the guffaws of his audience.

It was no great thing to do, perhaps; but it was admirably done. There was no extravagance in his accompanying actions, nor exaggeration of emphasis anywhere. In short, there was something of the genuine artist in him, and it was evident that he held his quaintly assorted 'tuppeny' audience in his grasp.

I grew strangely interested in the queer little figure before me. Something about him appealed strongly to the imagination.

He was encored again, and as I watched him more narrowly his aspect became more and more pathetic. I grew convinced that he was suffering physical pain; the blot of vermilion on his nose glowed brighter; beneath his mask of white I could see ashen-coloured lines streaking a colourless face.

'Poor little chap,' thought I; 'he's starving!'

Just at that moment he concluded at the 'wings,' bowing to the audience. His linen blouse blew open as he turned, and below a ragged shirt thus momentarily visible I saw that which made me suddenly feel sick. Before I recovered myself he had passed out on a step, humming his refrain, '*Oh, it makes me very, very lively!*'

Now, what I saw was a tumour which could only mean one thing, and that was death—an early and painful death probably. 'He's not starving,' I muttered to myself; 'poor little chap, he's dying!'

I thought I would go out into the fresh

air, but as I prepared to rise my eye caught sight of a chink in the canvas through which the 'green room' was visible.

The trapeze gentleman was now performing, and the clown was removing his 'make up.' Now that he was off the stage I could see that he had a limp. A gust of wind came suddenly, enlarging the opening. He turned, apparently to close the orifice; his eyes met mine, and in that startled second I knew him to be the 'Caleb Jay.'

Repressing a cry of surprise, I came out, and went round to the back to wait for him.

III.

'Now, tell me,' said I, as I led him up to the station, 'why do you do it? You know you oughtn't to, for it will kill you if you exert yourself like that.'

'Ay, an' that's why,' replied he, 'for I ken I'm dyin'; I went an' axed a doctor a while back, iv Oldcastle, an' he says, "I'll gie ye a year ti live at the ootside," says he.'

'Then, why do it?' I urged. 'Do you love it so, or is it for the sake of the money?'

'Ay,' he replied, gasping a little, as we mounted the slope to the station, 'that's it. It's for the brass.   Ye ken Tom, my brother? Well, it's for him i' pairt, an' i' pairt for my mother, who wants a bit frae me for my keep, ye ken.   Noo, Tom's a bonny fellow, ain't he?--just a joy ti the eye ti look upon ; an' he's aye wantin' a bit mair brass for this, an' that, an' t'ither, an', man, it's a pleasure ti me ti slave a bit for him.   There's nae use o' brass for me—me that' just the puir " Caleb Jay "—but Tom's like a live lord when he's plenty of brass ; an', man, but he spends it weel !'

I was silent for a while, thinking of the tragedy of it all.   Then I inquired again : 'Well, but how did you know you had this gift of acting and singing and impersona- tion ? and why did you hide your talent so carefully from us all ?'

'It came ower us first, I think,' he

answered, 'when reading Shakespeare an'
tragedies an' sic like.   I seemed ti see the
vary actors theirselves before my eyes, an' I
fair felt like them, ye ken.   Ye'll think it
strange, mevvies, but grandfeythor, he had
a bit talent that way, an' ran awa frae his
home, an' made his livin' play-actin', an'
piano-playin', an' singin', an aal.   He took
ill somewhere aboot here, an' died, an'
feythor, he took ti warkin' at the pits, an'
that's the story of it,' concluded my little
companion shyly.

'But with a gift like yours, why didn't you
tell *me* of it, for example, or the minister,
and perhaps we could have got you a proper
start somewhere?'

'Ay, I kenned that,' said he, 'an' thank
ye kindlies; but I found, on tryin' it, that I
wesn't strang enow for't iv a reg'lor way; an'
forbye that, I didn't want the laddies ti ken
aboot it, lest they might call us "Hamlet,"
mevvies, or "clownie," or sic like, an' my
mother divvent like play-actin'; it was she as

made my feythor give it up, sayin' it wes nae bettor than a mugger's* life, elwis wanderin' frae one place tiv anuther, an' nae brass iv it at aal.'

There was no time for further talk, for the train was waiting, and, arriving at our destination, I found my companion so tired that it was all he could do to walk home.

The minister and I put our heads together after this, and collected enough money to send our little friend down to a seaside home for a few weeks.

On Saturday night, however, a message came from the doctor that he was rapidly sinking. His mother and brother were both out, as it happened, but the minister and I arrived just in time to bid farewell to the poor little 'Caleb Jay.'

As we proceeded silently homeward, an idea came into my head.

'In an age of public testimonials and memorials,' I said, 'humble self-sacrifice

---

* 'Mugger'= beggar ; literally, one who sells mugs.

10

goes unrewarded. Our little friend ought to have a statue at the least; but, of course, it is no good doing anything. You, therefore, should bring him into your sermon to-morrow evening, and give a few people a hint of it beforehand.'

The idea seemed to strike my companion, and he said he would gladly do so.

I had not seen Tom, but as I walked to my lodgings I passed him standing at the street corner amidst a knot of companions.

I heard one of them mention the 'Caleb Jay,' and I stayed my steps a moment to hear the reply.

'Ay,' said Tom, 'he was a plucky little beggor iv his way, an' useful tae, an' I was often sorry for him, *he wes sae tarr'ble ugly!* But, ho-way, I's plenty brass on me, and I'll treat ye aal tiv anuthor beor!'

GEORDIE ARMSTRONG, 'THE JESU-YTE'

I.

GEORDIE ARMSTRONG, after a somewhat stormy past, had become a steady hewer, and a local preacher of some repute. Never a Sunday but he was 'planned' to speak at this or that village, and frequently, as he found opportunity, would 'pit in a bit overtime' at a 'class-meeting' or 'knife-an'-fork tea,' when the 'asking a blessing' or a returning of thanks might furnish occasion for a 'bit extemporizin'.' He was in receipt of excellent wages down the pit; his wordly goods comprised, as he often proclaimed, a 'bonny, an' what's o' far mair importance, a godly missus, three canny bairns, a cosy

10—2

hoos, a fine little librairee, an' a tarr'ble fertile garden.'

As he thought upon the sum of his blessings one Saturday night when, after having 'weshed hissel' an' had his tea,' he proceeded to light his pipe, he felt he could only properly describe himself as a ' varitable corn-u-cop-ye-ar ov happiness.'

Yet even then, even in that depth of felicity, an uneasy feeling would intrude: the memory of Scotty would float to the surface of his mind, and the thought of the 'parlous state' in which his old 'marrow' (mate) stood would ruffle its calm placidity.

This was 'the little rift within the lute'; here was the caterpillar in the ' corn-u-cop-ye-ar,' and, like the Apostle Paul of old, he was fain to accept his trial, in the spirit of true humility, as a judgment upon him for the failings of his past life.

It was not for lack of trying that Scotty refused to come to chapel ; indeed, Geordie had so vexed him with his importunity that Scotty had refused to work with him any longer, and was now employed further 'in-by' with another mate. But for all that, Geordie felt certain that the cause of failure lay with himself, due probably to his weakness in faith, to lack of some essential or other, and that the blame of Scotty's not being 'brought to the Lord' lay at his door.

It had been evident to him for some time that he must try other means, and, being a great reader, he had latterly come across, and been much attracted by, a remarkable account of some ancient methods of the 'Jesu-ytes' in cases of this sort.

Sometimes the sinner in question had been unwittingly tempted into the 'narrow path' by the gratification of his ambitions on some point or other, conversion resulting, as in the case of Tom Appleby — once a fire-hot Socialist, now a sleek Conservative—from unexpected prosperity.

At other times the same end had been

attained by a crafty flattery. Suppose a man ambitious of eminence and State distinction : he might be diverted from politics to the Church, and many were the instances given of bold and ambitious men who had done great work and attained high place as the servants of St. Peter.

Could Scotty not be caught hold of in some such fashion ? queried Geordie to himself, as he sat by his fireside that night, deeply pondering the records he had just been studying. 'I divvn't think he's ambitious, for he cares nowt aboot politics, an' he never even thought o' stannin' for election on wor Parish Cooncil. Aal he cares for is his beer, an' his quoits, an' bettin', an'—an'— his pansies ; an' I doot I cannot catch haud ov him in any one of those partic'lors, for it wouldn't be fittin' for us that's a local preacher to gan an' send him a barril o' beer, or back him at a quoitin' match. But stay—there's the pansies ; he's pansy champion, dootless ; but then I's leek champion, an' if I can grow leeks, I's warn'd but I can grow pansies, for flooers is easier grown nor vegetables.'

Geordie puffed at his pipe vigorously for a minute or two in silence as he turned the matter over in his mind.

A light kindled slowly in the back of his deep-set eye, a smile showed upon his lips, then he cuffed himself vigorously upon the knee.

' Ho-way, gan on, Geordie !' he encouraged himself aloud ; ' thoo's turnin a fair Jesu-yte, I's warn'd !'

*   *   *   *   *

As the day appointed for the annual meeting of the Flower Show drew near, Geordie had been heard to drop hints of the 'wonnerfu' new specie ' of pansies he had become possessed of—' seedlin's ' he had obtained ' doon the south-country way,' and it was not long before the rumour reached the ears of Scotty.

Nothing could exceed the contempt of

the latter when he heard of Geordie's trying to grow pansies—'him that's just a vegetable man, a tormut (turnip) grower, a sort o' ha'penny farmer,' and as for anything good in the way of seedlings coming out of the south-country, it was just 'bang ridi'klous,' for a' folk kenned that a' the best growers lived in auld Scotland.

By-and-by some mischievous individual told Scotty that Geordie was 'full' set upon being pansy champion, and was so cock-sure about it that he was willing to back himself to win.

Scotty was so annoyed at this that the next time he came across Geordie he could not refrain from jeering at his attempt at pansy growing. 'Wey, it'll be as muckle as ye can do to tell a pansy frae a vi'let!' he cried.

Geordie looked at him seriously from under his bushy eyebrows as he replied, 'I's gannin' to show—an' I's gannin' to win—*wi'' pansies, not vi'lets.*'

'Will ye back yorsel', then?' retorted his opponent sneeringly.

'Well, ye knaa,' replied the other slowly, with evident embarrassment, ' I's not a bettin' man, but if thoo thinks I's not in earnest, I's willin' to gie a proof that I is. What d'ye say to yor takin'—if ye beat us, that is—anythin' oot o' my hoos thoo has a fancy for ; an'— an'—if I beat thoo, wey, aal I axes is that thoo should come to chapel —noo an' again, ye knaa—ov an evenin',' he hastily added, as his companion's face assumed a look of infinite scorn.

'Ha' ye got that auld double-barrelled shot-gun yet?' queried Scotty, after a pause in which he had arrived at the conclusion that the odds were 'aboot a thoosand to one' in his favour.

'Yes,' replied Geordie.   'I still have her ; she's there hangin' up above the mantel-shelf.'

'Well, I'll tak' up wi' yor proposal,' was Scotty's reply.

'Shake hands on't, then,' said Geordie slowly, unsuccessfully endeavouring to instil an apprehensive tremor into his voice.

His companion shook hands carelessly, and swung away whistling barefacedly, 'And it's up wi' the bonnets o' Bonnie Dundee.'

Geordie, on his part, walked away swiftly homewards, fearing lest his exultation might betray itself too openly. 'Wow!' he thought to himself, 'but I's fair a-feard o' mysel'. I's growin' intiv a proper Jesu-yte!'

The morning of the show-day came, and Geordie, having finished packing his exhibits with extraordinary care, had just returned with the small cart the grocer had lent him to convey his treasures to the show-field, about a mile and a half distant, when up came Maggie, Scotty's wife, who, notwithstanding the little difference between their respective men, had always kept up her friendship with Geordie's wife. Her arms bore a large green case, tied round with a many-knotted cord. This she hastily set

down beside the cart, then turned breath-
lessly to Geordie, who, with his son, was just
about to drive off.

'Eh noo, canny man,' she cried, as she
wiped her hot face with the tail of her gown,
'do us a favour. Will thoo carry my man's
pansy-case up to the show wi' yors ? Wor
Jimmy was to have taken it up first thing
this mornin', but he went aff for his school
treat an' left it—an' my man's awa playin'
hissel' at quoits—an' he'll aboot kill Jimmy
when he gans up to the show an' finds his
pansies isn't there.'

Geordie willingly acceded, and the green
case was carefully deposited alongside of his
own at the bottom of the cart.

His nine-year-old son squatted on the seat
opposite, his legs up to his chin, so as to be
out of the way as much as possible in the
crowded cart. The pony started off gallantly
enough, and all went well till within about
two or three hundred yards of the field. At
that point, however, the pony suddenly shied

at some stray paper on the road, and Tommy fell with a crash upon the green case below.

'Eh, Tommy, lad!' cried his father in dismay ; 'what hast thoo done ? Wow! but thoo's gan an' smashed Scotty's case right thro' an' thro'!'

His succeeding feeling was one of joy ; for, the accident having irreparably damaged a third at least of his rival's pansies, it was evident that Scotty was now 'catched,' and Geordie, with an inward acknowledgment to Providence, saw, as in a vision, Scotty sitting devoutly 'under' himself in chapel.

A few moments later, however, doubt and dismay entered his soul. What if Scotty should say Tommy had done it ' o' purpose '— at his instigation ? Further reflection convinced him that this was exactly what Scotty would say, and doubtless there would be some folk unkind enough to back him up in it.

Scotty would likelies claim the gun.

Well, he'd not mind parting with that, but he could not give up the prospect of saving Scotty's soul alive without a groan.

'Eh, Tommy, lad! Eh, Tommy! But thoo divvn't knaa what thoo's done; thoo's put us in a fine quandary,' he murmured, gazing sadly now at Tommy, who was rubbing his knee ruefully, and again at the splintered case. The problem was a 'puzzlor;' even a Jesu-yte might have found solution difficult; for Scotty, he knew, would not believe him if he told the simple story of the accident, and winning the prize would be useless in the face of Scotty's insinuations of foul play.

The only way out of the difficulty, he determined sadly, was to exhibit his own pansies under Scotty's name, and withdraw from the contest himself. The contents of the two cases were sufficiently alike for his purpose, though his own were superior in size and depth of colour. It was a 'sair trial,' for his pansies were bound to win; but his character as an honest, religious man was at stake, and Scotty's triumph would be easier to endure than his sneers, if defeated, at a 'chap who caa's hissel' releegious, an' swindles ye like a Jew pedlar.'

With a groan he undid the label, and tied it on to his own beloved specimens, casting aside, as a temptation of the evil one, a disturbing suggestion that he was guilty of deception in passing off his own as Scotty's pansies.

*   *   *   *   *

The judges had been round, and Scotty's pansies easily gained the place of pride; pansies so perfectly developed, so dark and deep in colour, had never been shown before.

A crowd of admirers stood round. Scotty came lurching up, having evidently held a preliminary carouse in certain expectation of the championship, and, with a careless glance at his exhibits and the red card attached, cried triumphantly :

'Ay! an' whaur's that Geordie body noo,

wi' his brags an' a'? Wey, I'm tauld he daurna even exhibit his ain puir specimens by the side o' mine! Look at thae pansies, an' think o' him wi' his yaller sheep's tormuts tryin' to vie wi' me that's the auld established pansy champion! Ay, I'm that ower an' ower again; an' what's mair, I've win his gun. Wey, I'll gang an' fetch her awa at aince!'

So boasting, the proud champion reeled off in triumph, inadvertently knocking up against a silent looker-on, who was standing in melancholy guise against a tent-pole some little distance away.

One morning, a day or so after the flower-show, it chanced that Tommy was late for school, and, rounding a corner hurriedly, ran up against a big boy, who was sporting a pansy in his buttonhole. The big boy, who was Scotty's son, immediately proceeded to cuff him for his carelessness, and Tommy retorted by " calling "* his opponent and his family connections with a ready profuseness.

* Abusing.

'Wey, even that pansy thoo's sportin'
divvn't belong thoo, nor thy feythor nowther,
it's my dad's growin'; he showed his ain
pansies as Scotty's, 'cos Scotty's happened
an accident i' the cart. Feythor took them
up for yor mither, 'cos thoo had forgottened
them, an' to save thoo a strappin'; an'
feythor's pansy champion, and Scotty's nowt
but a beer-barril!'

'Liar!' responded the other boy, with a
punch of his fist.

'Ax yor mither, then,' shouted Tommy,
as he ducked and broke away from his
captor's clutch.

A night or two after this encounter Geordie
was surprised by a visit from Scotty.

'Whatten a tale's this ye're spreadin'
aboot o' yor showin' yoor pansies as mine,
I'd like to ken?' demanded the intruder
wrathfully.

Geordie looked up quietly from his book,
and: 'I've spread no tales aboot thoo or thy
pansies,' he replied.

'Weel, it's either thoo or that wee, impittent son o' yoors, Tommy.   Noo, I've
been axin' my missus aboot it, an' she says
she did gie ye my pansies to tak' up to
the show wi' yoors; an' what I want to be
at is what i' the deil's name ye did to them.'

Geordie, in reply, exactly related what had
occurred.

'Then, wey didn't ye tell us aboot it?'
demanded Scotty, still dissatisfied.

'Because thoo has a tarr'ble sharp tongue
i' thy mouth, an' I divvn't want to be scanda-
lized aboot the village as one who would
sharp another for the sake o' winnin' a floo'er
prize.'

'Hum!' ejaculated Scotty, 'it's an extra-
ordinar' thing this!   But hoo can ye explain
aboot the pansies, then?   I'm pansy champion,
an' therefore thae pansies that win the prize
mun ha' been mine, yet here ye are sayin'
that they were yoors.'

Geordie got up from his seat, and, without
immediately replying, went into the room at

II

the back, and came forth again bearing in his arms a shattered green case.

'Dis thoo recognise this?' he asked quietly, as he set it down on the table in front of his visitor.

'Ay,' replied Scotty, after a minute inspection; 'it's mine dootless.   But what then?'

'Wey, then, thoo has my case, an' my pansies inside ov it; an' here's yors still left i' their holes, just as they were on show-day.'

Scotty bent over the broken lid incredulously, lifted a faded specimen out, and regarded it contemptuously.

'Na, na,' he asserted shortly, 'that's no my pansies; mine were champions, an' these is weeny things.   Na, na, there's been a bit queer play about this.   Maybe Tommy changed them frae the one case to the ither.'

'Tommy did nowt o' the sort,' retaliated Geordie quickly.   'Aal that was done was to untie the label an' clagg (stick) it on to my case instead o' yors.'

'Weel, it's a dommed queer thing aal-tegither,' replied Scotty, pushing his cap from his brow, 'and beyont me; for I'm champion, nobody can deny that, an' a proper professor at floo'er growin', an' ye're but an ammytoor, d'ye see? An' it's just surprising to me that ye could e'er imagine ye could compete wi' me. But I divvn't wish to be ower hard on ye, an' I'll e'en gie ye the benefit o' the doot, as the saying is; sae I'll just send ye back yoor gun—that is,' he continued slowly, eyeing Geordie wist-fully, 'if ye're wishfu' to ha' her back.'

'Thoo can keep her,' replied Geordie, 'for it's nae use to me nowadays; but I would like—I would be tarr'ble pleased if thoo would come——' Here he halted abruptly, on a sudden fear lest Scotty's sus-picions of some underhand play in regard to the pansies might be again roused if he too openly requested him to come to chapel.

The other hesitated a little. 'Weel,' he said finally, 'it's a canny wee gun, an' I

11—2

would gey like to keep her. An' as for chapel gangin'—for I suppose that's what ye're after—if ye divvn't blab aboot us, wey, I'll just tak' a look in noo an' again.'

'That's right, noo,' responded Georgie gratefully, and his deep-set eyes glowed with a warmer light. 'Shake hands on't.'

Scotty shook hands without demur and swiftly departed, fearful lest Geordie might regret the arrangement.

Geordie leant back in his chair and heaved a sigh of relief as he offered up a silent thanksgiving to Providence for having softened Scotty's heart.

'It's aal right noo,' he murmured. 'Wi' the help I've had from above I've catched him at the finish, an' chapel will do the rest.'

Thus for some time he reflected devoutly. Then of a sudden a smile broke upon his lips and he clapped his hand vigorously upon his thigh. 'By!' he exclaimed aloud, 'but I's a proper Jesu-yte efter aal!'

'GEORDIE RIDE-THE-STANG'

The custom of 'riding the stang' is now obsolete, so that the date of this story must be put back a number of years, though Mr. Brockett,* writing in his glossary of Northumbrian words, in the early part of this century, says, 'I have myself been witness to processions of this kind. Offenders of this description are mounted a-straddle on a long pole, or stang, supported upon the shoulders of their companions. On this painful and fickle seat they are borne about the neighbourhood backwards, attended by a swarm of children huzzaing and throwing all manner of filth. It is considered a mark of the highest reproach, and the person who has been thus treated seldom recovers his character in the opinion of his neighbours.' The method of divination by the puddings has been practised within living memory, and even yet may be resorted to by way of a jest upon occasion.

Since writing the above the author has come across in Mr. R. Blakeborough's interesting book, 'Yorkshire Wit, Character and Customs,' a different version of 'riding the stang,' to which he is indebted for the first four lines of the 'furrinor's' song. In a footnote Mr. Blakeborough adds that the 'stang' was ridden at Thoralby, Wensleydale, as recently as October, 1896.

---

* Mr. Brockett died in 1842.

THERE was French blood in Geordie Robertson's wife, Mary, and it may perhaps have been owing to her origin that she was so eager for revenge when she found herself deceived by her husband.

She had begun to suspect him of infidelity even before a neighbour had given her a hint that he had a 'fancy' wife away in Bridgeton, for her husband brought home less and less with his 'pack' after his weekly tramp was over, and when she asked for explanations he 'called' her with most abusive virulence.

For her further satisfaction she determined to make trial, now that the pig was to be killed, of the ancient method of divination practised by the pit-wives, of which the following is the ritual:

When the animal has been slaughtered and the blood duly made into puddings, these puddings are 'set away' to boil by the inquirer of the oracle. Then, just before they are taken out of the 'pot,' the officiating priestess must say aloud that she 'gives them' to him who is suspected of infidelity. Should the puddings emerge whole, gossip is dumfoundered; should they come forth broken, the man is proved to have a 'fancy' wife.

Mary, indeed, found she could scarcely control her impatience when the fatal day came, and, the pig duly slaughtered, she 'gave' the puddings to her husband, Geordie.

She waited another minute to give the spell the lawful grace, then with a trembling hand plucked forth the puddings.

'Ah—ah!' she gasped, tremulous but triumphant, 'then it is so; he has a fancy wife,' and her quick brain fell to pondering a plan for discovery and revenge.

The first thing to be done was to lure her 'man' into a false security by subtle com-miseration with him on the 'slackness' of trade, as also by a wonderful submissiveness, even to the extent of going without bacon

for breakfast in order that she might save
enough to buy him tobacco.   Now this form
of procedure with a selfish man usually
produces excellent results.   If he is sufficiently selfish, he does not stay to inquire
why or wherefore, but takes all he can, as
a cat her cream, without delay, without a
thank you—nay, unlike tabby, without even
an inward purr.

It was so with Geordie, who began incontinently to brag about his 'missus's trainin','
and how he was 'champion' at 'fettlin' a
wife's nonsense,' and, swollen with self-satisfaction, began now to treat her with a sort of
contemptuous toleration.

A fortnight or so after Mary had made
trial of her puddings, Geordie carelessly
mentioned the fact that he would be away
over the 'week-end' in and about Bridgeton,
and demanded some 'brass' from her for the
replenishing of his 'pack.'

Outwardly submissive, she gave him five
shillings from her small savings, but inwardly

determined that it was the last sum of money he should have from her.

On Friday night Geordie departed gaily for Bridgeton, and on the Saturday afternoon Mary followed suit, clad in a thick cloak which might serve her for a disguise upon occasion.

When she arrived there, the main street and market were thickly crowded with a swarm of holiday-making pitmen, country folk, farmers and their wives, hinds, male and female, for it was the date of the annual fair and hiring, of 'the general assembly' of tramps, pedlars, 'tinklers' (tinkers), showmen, and the like, whose business it is to attend such gatherings.

In such a crowd Mary felt safe from recognition, but it might be a difficult task to discover her 'man' in all that company.

An hour or two passed, and she had been up and down the long street twice without success; but just as she was turning into a cheap refreshment-room, with 'Tea and coffy

always redy' written in a slovenly hand upon
a dirty placard in the window, she caught
the sound of a voice raised in semi-drunken
irritation close behind her which caused her
to turn her head hurriedly in that direction.

Yes, there he was without doubt, her
Geordie, heavy with liquor already—not
'mortal' yet, but quarrelsome. Aha! and
that was the 'fancy' wife, of course, who
had him fast by the arm—a blousy, red-
faced, fat-armed, big-chested woman, who
was evidently trying to persuade her charge
to come home much against his inclina-
tion. At sight of her rival — immodest,
gross, overpowering — Mary shrank back
aghast, and it was only after a struggle with
herself and a forcible iteration of her wrongs,
that she could persuade herself slowly and
reluctantly to follow the couple in front of
her.

'Ho-way!' shouted Geordie; 'there's Tom
Turnbull ower by there tryin' ti lift weights

an' show 's strength. Wey, but Tom cannet lift weights, he's nowt but a wee bit beggor. Tom, thoo beggor!' he challenged across the intervening throng of heads, 'thoo cannet lift weights; wey, Aa'l lift weights wi' thoo for a bottle o' whisky!'

'Ho-way, then, thoo aad fightin'-cock! but Aa give thoo fair warnin' Aa can beat thoo, for Aa's champion.'

At this, the 'fancy' wife seized her 'man' firmly by the sleeve, fearing doubtless lest, in his then 'muzzy' condition, Geordie would waste the scanty remainder of his brass upon a vain endeavour, and, by way of effectually dissuading him, indiscreetly praised his rival's prowess.

'No, no, Geordie, my man, come this way, an' give us my fairin'; wey, there's a mort o' things ti see yet; there's the shuttin'-gall'ry, an' the twa-headed cat, an' the giant, an' the fat woman, an' aal—ho-way. Ay, an' Geordie, hinny, Tom Turnbull's tarr'ble clivvor at liftin' they handles things an'

drivin' the bolt up the stick wi' the hammer,
an' Aa's warn'd but he'll bang thoo at that
game.'

'Tom Turnbull!—that haalf-grown, bandy-
legged beggor ov a bit tailor ov a man bang
me?   Gox! but Aa'll larn him a lesson.
Aa'll cut his comb, Aa's warn'd!' and Geordie
forthwith, murmuring maledictions, thrust
blindly through the crowd till he reached
the spot where his rival stood, the centre
of an admiring circle of friends.

'Noo,' cried Geordie, turning up his wrist-
cuffs, 'Aa'll show thoo hoo the thing's done
when it's done proper.   Wey, this bolt 'll
hit the beam at the top when Aa gie the
stump a bat!' and without more ado—amidst
the jeers of some, and the encouragement of
a few false friends—he seized the hammer,
swung it round his head, and brought it
down some feet wide of the mark—smash
upon the cobble-stones of the market-place.
'That's done the business!' cried Geordie
triumphantly, conscious from the stinging of

his hands that he had 'gi'en it a champion bat,' and certain that he had driven up the bolt some feet above his rival's mark.

Through the roar of laughter, which Geordie complacently accepted as the proper accompaniment of Tom's defeat, a voice pierced suddenly with a shrill note as of a fife.

'Thoo great clumsy lubbert, see what thoo's done! Thoo's broke the hammer's head off! That's half a crown, my man, for the hammer, an' a penny for the shot; an' if thoo disn't hand it ower, I'll call the pollis, for it's fair takin' the livin' oot ov a poor weeda woman's mouth to break her hammer thet fashion!' and a thin-faced female, with a red-lined nose, sharp cheekbones, and watery eyes, held up two skinny fists in anger against him.

'Gan on, woman, gan on!' retorted Geordie indignantly; 'wey, it's thoo sh'd pay us, or gie us a cigyar, or a cokienut; for that bat o' mine hit the bull's-eye, Aa's warned.'

The shrill-voiced female renewed her pro-
testations, and some of the bystanders joined
in with additional explanations; but Geordie
would have none of them. 'Gan on,' he
retorted; 'gan awa home, an' wesh yor
feyce! Wey, the hammer's as rotten as
pash, for Aa brought her fair doon like a pick
reet on top o' the stump. What else should
maa hands be tinglin' for?'

The proprietress of the hammer, however,
continued to assail Geordie with abuse, while
at the same time the 'fancy' wife upon his
other side endeavoured to drag him away, so
that it need not surprise us if Geordie
suddenly lost his temper, and turned heavily
upon his tormentors.

He shook off the one, and flung down a
shilling in payment of the supposed damage
to the hammer; the other—the 'fancy' wife
—he pushed roughly from him, with the
result that she lost her balance, and fell
whimpering in the mud, while Geordie
lurched off to the nearest hostelry, muttering

indignantly as he went, 'Aa's been fair mucked ower wi' women the day—just fair mucked ower.'

A swift inspiration gleamed in Mary's mind. For the punishment of Geordie she had already made due preparation, and now, if she could only persuade the 'fancy' wife, her triumph would be complete.

She noticed the woman angrily brushing the muck off her 'feast gown,' and at once made her way up to her and touched her gently on the arm. 'Ay,' she said quietly, as the other looked up with red and testy face, 'an' it's the same way he treats me;' holding her left hand loosely so that her marriage-ring was plainly conspicuous.

'So he has a lawful wife, an' yore her?' And the speaker gave a suspicious, all-embracing stare. 'Well,' she continued slowly, jealousy slipping, like some slow portcullis, from her eyes, 'he's had a change, has my lord! Forst, it was a thin lass like yorsel', an' noo it's a plump one like me.

Ay, he's greedy, is Geordie ; he winna be content wi' the one, like Jack Spratt, but wants both.'

'Ay, lass,' replied the other woman quietly, ' yore right : he's greedy an' selfish.   That's the sort—a selfish good-like nowt, that lives on women, makes them keep him through life just as one does a babby ; an' he's treated the pair ov us shameful—just shameful ; but, hinny, I've a plan for a bit payment for him, an' if ye come aside a bit wi' me, I'll tell ye o't.'   And she laid an appealing hand upon the other's, and affected with the disengaged one to brush the remaining dirt from the ' fancy ' wife's skirt.

' Well, what is't ?' said the latter, suffering herself to be led through the crowd to a quiet corner.

Mary at once proceeded, but with a cautious self-effacement, to detail her schemes for Geordie's discomfiture.   ' It will not hurt him,' she protested, as her rival still sat silent, ' but it will pay him a bit for the way he's treated us'—here Mary's hand again occupied itself with the soiled dress—'and it will give ye the laugh over him. I've done wiv him mysel ; I'm awa to France to-night or morning—that's where Grandfeyther was bred ; he came to these parts selling onions at first, an' finally settled doon here to 'scape the soldierin'. An' I've money enough to pay the expenses,' she continued ; 'an' for suthin' to eat an' drink an' the ticket.'

The 'fancy' wife looked at her somewhat hardly, suspicion rising to the surface of her eye. 'An' sae yore off to France, are ye?' she queried ; 'ay, an' yore tired ov him ? Well, mevvies he would say as he was tired o' thoo ; but I've a grudge again' him for the way he's treat us to-day, spendin' aal my brass ower himsel' an' clartin' my gown an' all, an' I'll pay him for't, I's warn'd.' And her face darkened vindictively.

'That's right,' replied Mary swiftly. 'And now for the plan. Here's money for you to

treat him with. Get him awa oot o' the
public before he's had too much, an' bring
him along wi' you by the last train from
Bridgeton, an' I'll meet you wi' the "stang"
ready for him, an' the lads, an' the music, an'
all. Oh, but it'll all gan fine, ye-es, ye-es!'

So Mary, having handed over all that she
could spare to her rival, departed for the
railway-station with a view to catching an
earlier train, and revising her preparations at
the other end.

Her elation was complete. The only
possible flaw in her subtly-devised plan lay
in the moods of the 'fancy' wife. If Geordie
continued to treat her roughly—and as he had
now evidently settled down to the drink, he
was almost certain to do so—she would be
true to the arrangement; if not, she might
relent, and keep Geordie from his house that
night.

*   *   *   *   *

The train was overdue, and Mary waited
with a feverish expectation at the station's

descent amidst a small crowd of young men and boys to whom the idea of making anyone 'ride the stang' had appealed with an irresistible sense of novelty.

The custom, indeed, was obsolete, but all had heard of it, and the older men had often witnessed it in their youth, and some of them had collected near the station to criticise and superintend the performance.

The 'stang' itself was in readiness—having been lent to Mary on this occasion by the schoolmaster and antiquary of the village, whose father had been, as constable, its custodian in the old days.

And now at last the rumble of an approaching train was audible, and the group at once assumed an alert and eager air.

A crowd of tired excursionists slowly descended the narrow path from the station, men and women together, but there was no sign of Geordie or the 'fancy' wife. Mary's heart grew heavy within her; after all, then, she would have to depart without that sweet morsel—her revenge. The 'fancy' wife must have relented and informed Geordie of her plans.

' Ho-way,' cried a man in her ear, ' he's not comin' back the night ; thoo's gi'en him a gliff mevvies.'

' Stay !' cried she swiftly, detaining him by the arm. ' What's that, then ?' she whispered triumphantly, as at the tail of the procession of pleasure-seekers a couple became visible descending fitfully with wayward lurches.

' See there !' continued Mary eagerly, ' it's Geordie an' his "fancy" wife with him. Catch tight haud of him, an' mount him, an' carry him through the length o' the village on the "stang"—right to his very door ; he canna get in though, for I've the key i' my pocket,' and Mary laughed with an inward glee.

Down came the couple slowly, Geordie abusing his companion, as he lurched against her heavily, for not progressing with more even footsteps, the woman saying nothing, but tightly gripping him by the arm, in order, doubtless, to keep him upright and also to prevent any attempt at escape.

The wicket-gate swung open, Geordie lurched through, and in a moment he was seized, hoisted into the air, a rough pole thrust through his legs, and the triumphal march began to the tune of a penny whistle, played by the local champion, a carter to trade, and a number of Jews' harps and toy trumpets with which a herd of small boys poured forth discordant revel.

'Gox! Aa's fallen intiv a sorcus (circus),' cried Geordie, in the first moment of astonishment, then, 'Leave haud ov us, ye great flamin' Irish—— What the devil's this Aa's astride o'?' adding with solemn dignity, 'Yore makin' a tarr'ble mistake. Aa's not Blondin, ti walk on a tight rope for ye ; Aa's Geordie Campbell o' the Raa (Row), whe lives i' the hoos wi' the brass handle tiv't.'

'Ay, ay, we knaa thoo !' cried the chorus of urchins ; 'thoo's Geordie, drunken Geordie,

Geordie wi' the "fancy" wife. Geordie, Geordie ride-the-stang! Eh, what a clivvor rider is Geordie! Thoo's a proper jockey, Geordie, an' thoo'll mevvies ride the winner i' "the Plate"* before thoo's finished wiv it.'

This idea tickled the carriers of the 'stang,' and Geordie's bearers were forthwith transformed into thorough-breds with a tendency to buck-jump. Hither and thither he rolled, dazed and bewildered, helplessly clutching at the heads of those near him for support, but his arms were seized, his legs tightly crossed below the 'stang,' and he swung from side to side, while the rougher boys, chanting rude doggerel over him, gathered and threw mud upon him. A trombone and a 'sarpint' here joined the noisy crowd, and to the varied strains of 'The Campbells are coming,' 'Weel may the keel row,' and 'Canny Dog Cappie,' Geordie was borne in triumph up the Row.

A 'furrinor' (foreigner, stranger) here joined

* The Northumberland Plate.

the medley, a 'South countryman' from Yorkshire, who, chancing to have lately come to
the village after some private experience of
his own in stang-riding in one of the remoter
Yorkshire vales, at once placed his services
at the crowd's disposal.

Marching at the head of the procession,
like the drum-major of a band, and beating
together two saucepan-lids, he led the
anthem.

Between the 'cling, cling, cling' of the
lids his voice rose lustily :

> 'Ah tinkle, ah tinkle, ah tinkle tang,
> It's not foor your part nor mah part
> 'At ah ride the stang,
> But foor you, Geordie Robertson, who his wife
>   did bang.'

Scarcely had he ended when the shrill
trebles of the boys took up the wondrous
tale, and in antiphony chanted their response :

> 'Up wiv a bump and down wiv a bang
> Gans Geordie, Geordie ride-the-stang :
> A bump an' a bang for his deed sae wrang,
> An' we'll larn him a lesson for ever sae lang.'

Then, to the full chorus, with complete

orchestra of flute and fife, trombone and triangle, tin whistle and 'sarpint,' brass pot, pan, and saucepan-lids, the entire procession moved slowly onward.

Mary's eyes burned bright with exultation as she marched along in the crowd, not letting a single incident of the spectacle escape her notice, and as she watched she too joined in the chorus of 'Geordie, Geordie ride-the-stang' without restraint.

The sound of the familiar voice roused the victim from the stupor into which the hustling, peltings, and shoutings had reduced him.

'Thoo ——,' he yelled, as he caught sight of her; 'then it's thoo that's at the bottom o' this?   By, but if Aa wes free Aa'd——' But a stalk of cabbage thrown at a venture by a small boy on the skirts of the crowd here impeded his utterance, and Mary's voice rang out perhaps more triumphantly than before.

The 'fancy' wife, meanwhile, who had at

first discreetly retired from public view and looked on at the procession from a distance, had shortly after joined the noisy throng, moved thereto by a sense of isolation, and also by a certain smouldering compunction. She looked around her irresolutely ; she felt she had acted precipitately ; certainly she was not deriving any advantage from the proceedings, whereas her rival was the leader of the revelry, dancing, clapping her hands, and carrying on like a ' Maypole lass.'

At this moment Mary inadvertently brushed against her, and in a moment the ' fancy ' wife turned upon her like a spitfire. Clenching her fists and shouting vituperations, she tried to seize her by the hair. Foiled in this by an adroit swerve of Mary's under the 'stang,' she turned her fury upon Geordie's bearers, and with such success that to defend themselves they were forced to lower the pole to the ground. ' Noo, Geordie,' cried she, promptly thrusting the wooden weapon into his hands, ' mak' play

wiv it, my man, ho-way,' and Geordie, realiz-
ing he was now free, lunged furiously in all
directions, and scattered the crowd like chaff
before him.

Steered by his 'fancy' wife, a way grew
clear about them, and Geordie marched
slowly, unsteadily forward, bearing the
'stang' like a battering-ram straight in
front of him, down the remaining length of
the Row, accompanied at a respectful distance by a rabble of the smaller urchins.

Right on past his house he went, out into
the darkness beyond, and over the bridge
at the end of the village, still tightly grasping
the 'stang' himself, and tightly grasped in
his turn by his 'fancy' wife.

The last train to Oldcastle happened to
pass above the bridge at that moment, and
a head leant far out through a carriage
window.

'Ay!' a clear voice sounded, with a touch
of derision on the night air—'Ay! that's
right, haud him tight, for he wants it badlies.'

YANKEE BILL AND QUAKER JOHN

QUAKER JOHN was one of the best known figures in the small seaport town of Old Quay.   Short of stature, heavy of tread, always quietly attired in a black suit, which varied not in cut from year to year ; indeed, the same suit had once been known to do duty for three years together, till his wife one day, so 'twas said, handed them over to the chimney-sweep in mistaken identity. You might have told that he was of Puritan descent some yards away, but the ' letter of the law ' in him had been softened down by the kindly genius of the old-fashioned Quaker. A genial twinkle lay in hiding at the back of his steadfast eye, and a smile was always ' at heel ' beside his big and honest mouth.

A broad and spectacled nose completed
the portrait of one in whom the harmlessness
as of a dove did not of necessity efface the
wisdom of the serpent.   At least, so said
Yankee Bill, who read character 'at sight';
but then, Bill was a disciple of that cynical
logic which proclaims not only all priests to
be humbugs, but all men immersed in business who make pretensions to piety to be
hypocrites or fools.

He had happened to pass along the street
one 'fourth-day' morning as John came out
of the meeting-house, and overheard him
address a remark about business to a Quaker
friend at his side, and thereafter was merci-
less in ridicule.   'John's patent incubator,'
he styled the meeting-house, 'for plot-hatch-
ing,' and pretended to be afraid of doing
business with him on Wednesday afternoons
for fear of being 'skinned.'

Bill was a waif from the seas who had
somehow been thrown up at Old Quay a few
years back, and having 'prospected around'

and 'pegged out a claim' for himself in the
indiscriminate region of commission business,
life insurance, advertising agencies, secretary-
ships, and other nebulous formative pro-
cesses, was now almost as well-known a
figure in the town as Quaker John himself.

The chief foundation in any abiding friendship is a certain diversity of temperament
which those who wondered at the mutual
liking that had sprung up between the re-
tiring stockbroker's clerk and the worldly
Yankee had evidently overlooked. To John
the American's audacity was a perpetual
delight, tempered by occasional Puritan
scruples as to whether he was justified in
associating with so hardened an unbeliever.
To Bill Coody the Quaker's reposefulness
and quiet self-sufficiency were both a sleep-
ing-draught and irritant.

Nothing delighted him more than to get a
rise out of John ; but John was hard to catch,
and even when craftily inveigled into a

theological argument, was extremely chary
of entering into definite statements. Even
when his position was most hotly assailed
by the other, who made unsparing use of
the *argumentum ad hominem*, reinforced by
a store of malicious anecdotes of religious
'professors' all the world over, John never
lost his temper, but mildly suggested that his
antagonist was an Anarchist in disguise.

John himself, though immersed in business
which some of the 'plain people' have been
used to look askance at, lived after the simple
fashion of the straiter sect.

After his day's work at the office, where as
head clerk much responsibility lay on his
shoulders, he would go straight home and
employ his leisure on fine days in his garden,
and on wet days in his library, for John
was not only a book-collector, but also a
reader.

One pipe of tobacco he allowed himself
before going to bed on week days and two
on 'first-days,' and flavoured his tobacco with

a chapter of 'George,' as he styled in affectionate intimacy his favourite author (Mr. Meredith) on week-days, but a portion of Barclay's 'Apology' on 'first-day' evenings.

One evening John was sitting reading as usual, when the maid-servant came in to say that Mr. Coody wished to have a few words with him. 'Very well,' replied her master, laying aside 'George' with a sigh, and wondering what business Bill might have on hand to come at such an untimely hour.

In came his friend as unceremoniously as ever, and, sitting himself down on the sofa, drew vigorously at his cheroot for a minute or two before entering upon the topic that had brought him thither.

'Look here, John,' he exclaimed all at once, 'you're a confidential cuss, I guess, and I've got a scheme on hand that will "scoop the boodle" if properly carried out; and what I want to know is, whether your people will take a hand in it or no. It's a certain thing, and will go ahead like a runaway buggy anyway; but the less friction the better, so that if your people will grease the wheels a bit, so much the better for them and all consarned.'

'Tell me precisely what it is,' replied John cautiously, 'then I may be able to offer an opinion; but, of course, I can't say off-hand whether the firm will entertain the idea or not.'

'Waal,' replied Bill, 'I guess you're the firm pretty often, for your bosses are generally away huntin' or shootin' or foolin' around somewhere; anyway, your advice is generally listened to, I guess. Waal, to come to business. I'm fixin' up a new store on the most modern principles. I sell everything cheaper than anybody else anywhere in this little country of yours; any bloomin' thing that's asked for, why, it's there, delivered free to any part of the United Kingdom. Every-body comes along—Noah's Ark on a wet day ain't in it for the pushin' there'll be at our doors once we get opened out—and, another thing, everybody gets made into an automatic shareholder ; for profits have to lie till they reach £5, when each man, woman, and child gets a share given them, will they, nill they—and you bet, John, they will. I tell you, the thing's fixed up, and is goin' to give Old Quay shocks. Why, I'm buyin' up here and there bankrupt stocks enough to bust the place with—pianners, hardware, bicycles, rose-trees, fam'ly Bibles, rat-traps—every taste will be suited, for I tell you cosmopolitanism ain't in it with Bill Coody. I tell you I'll be in a position to bust every single bicycle dealer in this little one-hoss place ; every pianner dealer can shut up shop when I get started. Why, there won't be a pitman in Northumberland who hasn't got a demi-grand Eureka B. C. piano in his house in another three weeks' time, and every colliery village will have its Bayreuth Festival with "Canny Dog Cappie" and "Weel may the keel row" tinklin' away down each row.'

13

'But think of the poor shopkeeper!' John interrupted, aghast at this slaughter of the innocents.

'Now, John,' expostulated Bill, as one who reproves a child for foolishness, 'it's not "first-day," and you ain't "in meeting," so stick to business, if *you* please. Waal, the thing's got to go, as I'm sayin', and the only question is, are your people goin' to join in or no? If not, I bust their little donkey go-cart of Supply Stores which they set up a few years back in South Street "for the mutual encouragement of thrift and the supply of the best articles at first-hand cost" as the prospectus says, combinin' philanthropy and five per cent. plus their commission on floatin' the shop. Now, I know how much they have in it, your bosses. J. B. has 10,000 shares, and young T. he has 5,000 out of a total of 30,000, so they're the largest shareholders in the concern, but Bill Coody has shares in it, too, John, he or his nominees. Likely you've noticed the shares have been

jumpin' up a bit lately and been wonderin'
what the jooce was up, eh?'

'Yes,' responded John quietly, endeavouring to conceal any disquietude he might feel;
'yes, I've noticed that.'

'Waal, we've got enough to bust their
shop up pretty well, and if your people don't
come into my showyard I'll give their shares
away with a pound of tea,' and here he pulled
out a handful of certificates from his trousers'
pocket and flourished them in John's face,
which was gradually growing longer as the
other unrolled his arguments.

'But how did you get the necessary
capital?' John inquired after a pause, professional curiosity piqued at this unexpected
revelation of means.

'Waal,' replied the American, as he carelessly lit another cheroot, expectorating with
relish into John's carefully-trimmed fire, 'I'll
tell you straight out, for I'm one of them
that goes straight to the point—fibbin' ain't
in it with truthfulness, and bluffin's no good

when the cards are on the table. Waal, I
bank with the Old Bank here, and decent
enough people they are, too, but a trifle slow,
so no sooner did the Joint Stock Bank open
out a new branch in Old Quay than in I go,
and I says, " Look here, boss, I want £5,000
of the ready, and I'll bring you business," I
says.   Well, the boss rubs his hands in
butter, and he says, " Sartinly, sartinly,
Mr. Coody, we know your name well, sir ;
most happy to oblige, I'm sure, and much
obliged if you could introduce us to a few of
your friends," so after a bit more palaver and
a deposit of some shares the deal's done.
Waal, down the street goes Bill Coody, and
into the parlour of the Old Bank, and says
to the partners straight out : " Now, look
here, gentlemen, there's no beatin' about the
bush with me, and no frivolity in matters of
business, and what I want is £5,000 straight
down, which is the figure I've just been
offered by the new Joint Stock Bank over
the way.   Now I like your style," I says,

"and I should be sorry to leave you; but sentiment's not my style of doin' business, so there you have it." Wall, the old gentleman looked at me over his spectacles, same way as you do, John, and under his spectacles also, and offers me a pinch of snuff, while he and his partner waggle their heads together in a far-off corner of the room. Waal, after a bit more palaver and a little "pi" jaw thrown in gratis about the evils of speculatin', and a hope that a strange bank will not interfere with mutual friendly business relations, that deal's done, and Bill Coody has £10,000 to draw upon by feedin'-time that morning.

'Waal, John, I think you'll have the hang of it now, and will be able to advise your bosses as to what's best for them and the community, too, at large, and I want an answer—a regular business-like document—signed, sealed, and delivered, by this time to-morrow night, for there's a shipload of my goods in already and lyin' at the quay, and I can't let the thing dry-rot while two

thickheads worry the situation out and try
to tinker up a mind between them. So fix
it up for them, John, yourself. Ta-ta; I
must be off. There's a chap waitin' for me
at the club on business.' And rising as
he spoke, he went as unceremoniously as
he came, leaving a trail of rank tobacco
that was as penetrating to John's nostrils
as his communications had been to his intellect.

John lit his pipe again, which had gone
out as he listened to Bill's scheme, and
thought for a while how 'George' would have
dealt with the situation; how his penetrating
intellect would have pierced through Bill's
armour - plating, and revealed the naked
artificer within.

Ah! if 'George' had only been there for
five minutes, several of the questions that
were troubling him might have received
instant solution. He could not feel certain
how far Bill meant business with his store.
It was not all bluff, of course; but how much

of it was bluff, how much business, he could not of himself determine.

It might be that he wanted to be bought off at a price, or be offered a post upon the directorate, or was merely a 'bull' of the shares. However, one thing was certain : there must be no shilly-shallying. Either Bill must be squared or he must be defied.

That was the question for him to determine. No doubt, from a strictly business point of view, the chief matter to be considered was which of the two courses was likely to prove most beneficial to his principals ; but the thought of the poor shopkeepers was present in John's mind, and operated largely in influencing his mind in the direction of defiance. There was poor old Mrs. S——, for example, who kept herself and two grandchildren on the proceeds of a small florist's business, once her son-in-law's. What would happen to her if Bill were to flood the town with rose-trees at a shilling the dozen ?

To-morrow was Saturday, and Bill demanded an answer by the evening. The next day being 'first-day,' he would have to satisfy his conscience—that 'still small voice' which, even in the silence of the meeting, interrogated him severely on his dealings during the past week, and permitted no subterfuge or evasive answer—and it was useless to think he could do so by pleading that he was only a subordinate, not an official, in this affair of the store. Well, so be it. It must be defiance, then—war to the knife—if Bill was in earnest; for to offer to put him on the directorate of the supply stores would merely mean setting up Bill's store under the old title.

John sat late as he pondered over the situation. Suddenly one of the Articles of Association of the stores flamed within the chamber of his brain, and a twinkle shone in his eye, as he reflected that it should enable him to mate Bill's cleverness at the very outset.

Bill had quoted from the prospectus, but

he had evidently overlooked the Articles of Association, and John chuckled to himself delightedly as he recalled Article 5.

Shortly after seven next morning John might have been observed taking the air upon the quay, casting shrewd glances as he passed along. He had some suspicions concerning the amount of value of Bill's consignment of pianos, family Bibles, etc., and he thought he might possibly discover something for himself if he saw what vessels were lying at the quay.

There was a green-hulled brigantine from Norway lying alongside, but she was full of battens and pit-props ; a steam-collier lay next, but she must simply be waiting there for stores or sailing orders. A tramp came next, apparently from America, by the labels on some of her packages that the cranes were already swinging overhead.

This, then, must be Bill's consignment, for there was nothing else in the river or at the quay that John could see that could possibly have anything on board for Bill or his stores.

As he stood there immersed in thought, a figure appeared on the deck above him, and, leaning his arms on the taffrail, regarded the scene below him with a gloomy air. 'The skipper,' thought John, as he noted his blue broadcloth and peaked cap, and on the spur of a sudden inspiration immediately accosted him.

'Fine morning, captain. I happen to have heard a rumour to the effect that you were wanting an offer for your cargo. If so, I might possibly get you an offer from a friend of mine—at a reasonable figure, of course.'

'Waal,' replied the other slowly, 'I guess I'm ready for a deal, as the consignees are bust up, and only 25 per cent. of the freight paid for ; but it's not a knock-out, I tell ye, for I've had a bid already for the lot.'

'Was it from a man they call Bill Coody, by any chance ?' asked John, with a fine carelessness.

'Waal,' replied the skipper, as he turned his quid, 'his name's nothin' to me, so long as he has the ready. Mr. Cash is the gent I do business with; but if my memory sarves me right, I think Bill Coody was the name on his pasteboard.'

'What precisely is the cargo?' queried John. 'Is it dry-store goods—organs, pianos, and such like commodities?'

'Ay, that's about what it is—all the sort o' fixin's that make a harmonious home for the retired commercial gent—organs, melodeons, brick-a-bacs, articles of virtoo and amusement combined; and a fine variety of wood goods besides. Waal, if you're for a deal you must be sharp about it, for I've to fix up with Mr. Coody by ten o'clock this mornin', and I leave again this afternoon, havin' just signed a fresh charter party for a cargo of fireclay bricks. So name your figure, plank down the cash, and I'm ready to deal.'

'Well, what did Mr. Coody offer you?' asked John pertinently.

'Three hundred pounds in bank notes,' replied the skipper; 'but I'll take £400 to clear; and dirt cheap, too, when you think o' what a nest o' nightingales your fam'ly and friends will be at ten dollars a head.'

'Thank you,' said John, as he moved away; 'I'll just go round and have a talk with my friend, and will let you know the result before ten o'clock.'

'Right,' replied the captain, cutting himself a fresh plug of tobacco; '£400 down, coin o' the realm, before ten, mind ye, and your friend's set up for life with a "house beautiful" that Solomon in all his glory and Mrs. Sheba couldn't have fixed up better between them.'

'What a curious, profane, hard-featured set of men these Americans are!' thought John, as he stepped briskly away in the direction of his senior partner's house. 'Why, the mind of that skipper is exactly of the same temper as Bill's; his features are as irregular, even his voice has the same twanging, nasal habit. However, he means business evidently, and I think I can persuade Mr. William to buy up his cargo, which will put, I imagine, a pretty stiff spoke in Bill's wheel.'

Within a quarter of an hour John was on Mr. William's doorstep, and ten minutes afterwards was explaining the strategical position to the senior partner in his dressing-gown. 'Certainly, John,' said Mr. William slowly, after listening attentively to John's recital; 'we couldn't possibly have Coody on our Board; it wouldn't do at all. Why, he's a mere adventurer, and his method of under-cutting, "busting" people up, etc., would bring discredit upon our firm and have a bad effect upon our business. No, it's quite evident, John, as you say, that we can't square him—as to how far he means business, I don't know. I incline to think he is bluffing us; but there isn't time to find out how much he has up his sleeve; and if we buy up this cargo we trump his ace, you think, and can make a profit out of it ourselves at the stores after? Well, I daresay you're right, John; and, after all, £400 won't ruin us. We buy his cargo, and as he can't "bear" the shares, he'll be like a chained dog showing his teeth, but doing no damage. Yes, I think it is an excellent idea, John,' Mr. William said in conclusion, 'and if you'll wait one minute I'll give you the cheque for £400.'

By ten o'clock that morning John had completed his defences; the cargo was bought; he held an indemnity against any claims from the skipper and owners of the goods in question; he had made an inquiry at the Old Bank, and now was sitting down at the office to write a short note marked 'private' to Bill, to tell him it was to be 'war to the knife.'

'And I may tell thee, Bill, that thee had better give in with a good grace; for, in the first place, thee cannot sell the shares below par—*vide* the Articles of Association, paragraph 10—and, in the second, we have bought up thy cargo; and, finally, I feel assured that stores managed on thy suggested lines would never bring a blessing with them. Thou saidst it was to be "war to the knife," but we hope thee will think better of it, for thy sake more than for our own,' and with a friendly warning John finished his letter, and despatched it by hand to 'William Coody, Esq.'

Late that afternoon, just as John was leaving the office, a letter was brought to him in Bill's handwriting. It ran as follows :

'Ta-ta, John, I'm off, you quaint, cocked-hat old Puritan Precisian ; but I couldn't leave without having tried a fall with you first, and, on totting it up, I think Bill Coody's just had a trifle the best of the mêlée. If I'd got on to the stores, I'd have stayed in this derned little one-hoss place, but those all-fired articles* upset that cart.

* 'Article 5.—No shares shall be dealt in below their face value except with the consent of the Board of Directors.'

I'll allow you that, John; but I have you, my boy, over that little cargo of mine. Why, the whole show was a got-up job, the cargo saw-dust, salvage stocks worth £20 at an outside figure. The skipper, being a pal of mine, lent me his duds, this morning, for I knew you'd be down there sniffing and spectacling about with the morning's sunrise, and I had the show ready for you, John, to walk into, and in you walked like blue blazes. The £400 will about pay for my trouble, and for the premiums on the store shares. Your principals will have to buy the shares back from the banks—they mustn't buy below par, though, John—you remind them of that.

'I've sold my biz., and am off with my pal, the skipper, this moment. No time to hand-shake. Ta-ta, John, and bear no malice. Stick to piety and 5 per cent., and don't buy up bankrupt cargoes, and you'll be Lord Mayor of Old Quay before you're finished. So long, your pardner,

'BILL COODY.'

THE PROTÉGÉ

THE Vale of the Frolic in the far west of
Northumberland had always been a
favourite retreat of mine. As I trudged the
London pavements in the dog-days before
the Law Courts rose, my heart panted for
the green hills and the sweet silences of
remotest Frolicdale.

The chiefest charm of the vale perhaps for
me lay in the fact that it was a track un-
trodden by the tourist, resembling the maid
of the waters of Dove in this—that it was
one which, as yet, there were 'few to know,
and very few to love.'

It was a pastoral, sheep-raising countryside, inhabited by shepherds almost entirely,
who were at the same time farmers also, for

their tenure was something after the métayer order.

There was nothing to mar the quaint and antique flavour of existence. The post, like our lifeboat institution, was here supported by voluntary contributions. If anyone were 'gannin' up the wattor,' well and good ; he would take the letters with him. If not, then they were left at the schoolmaster's till called for. Newspapers, again, with the exception of a weekly *Courant* or a *Scots Mail*, were, like the woodcock, but ' occasional visitors' in that region ; and when it is added that the house I usually stayed at was situated eighteen miles from a terminus of a slow branch line of the North British Railway Company, it will be evident that the ordinary tourist had a very poor chance of putting in an appearance in that favoured region.

I was recalling all these little details with infinite gusto as I sat down at my desk to write to my friend the Presbyterian minister and schoolmaster of Fair-Green Haugh, suggesting a visit from myself a week ahead.

The answer came just in time for me to pack up and start within the week.

'I am sorry to say,' wrote my friend in conclusion, 'that my accommodation is somewhat limited this summer, as I have had to give up my small sanctum to a protégé of mine, who, though he has just been discharged from gaol, will yet, I feel assured, become a highly useful and respectable member of society.

'I know your kind heart, my friend,' he continued, 'and feel sure you will not regret a temporary lack of comfort in so good a cause. You can always use the schoolroom, as it is holiday time, for reading, writing and smoking.'

'Heavens!' I murmured to myself, as I took in the monstrous situation; 'fancy having to spend my vacation trying to improve an infernal burglar! He knows

my kind heart, he says.   Well, it only
proves the truth of the poet's lines :

> ' " Not e'en the dearest heart, and next our own,
>   Knows half the reasons why we smile or cry."

I wonder,' I soliloquized, 'whether he is
of the heavy, hang-dog, dropped-jaw type
—the knifing variety, in brief—or the other
species—the shifty-eyed, chinless, quick but
evil brained sort.   On the whole, I prefer the
first, for if he cannot control his temper, at
any rate you know where you are with him,
whereas with the latter you never can tell
what he may be up to.'

Anyway, it was exasperating, for here had
I been congratulating myself upon the sweet
security of my proposed retreat, only to discover at the last moment that I was destined
to become co-warder of a criminal.

However, it was no use making myself
miserable before the time, and as I was at any
rate now free from the choking London atmosphere I could revel in the thought of fresh
country air, liberty and leisure.

I stayed the night at Heathtown (famous for the church wherein Bernard Gilpin, 'the apostle of the north,' stayed the hot Borderers from feud), and, drawing the heather-honeyed air deep into my lungs, felt my strength so renewed that the thoughts of shifting the ticket-of-leave gentleman if he didn't. in North-country phrase, 'keep a civil tongue in his heid and behave hissel' respectable,' positively inspired me with pleasure.

The postman in his cart was, as it chanced, going up to the little village, styled a 'toon,' where the last post and telegraph-office this side of Scotland is situated, and insisted upon giving me a 'cast' so far upon my road.

'No, nowse is changed ava,' he replied, in answer to my query, 'syne ye were last here, save belikely that we are aal a year older, an' that Farmer Newton's missus was brought tae bed wi' anither bairn a month ago last Saterday. Ye'll mind she had her fourth bairn the last time ye were here, an' Farmer Newton, he says he'll just hae tae turn priest, an' get the Sixstanes livin',* an' there, ye ken, the Queen sends ye a ten-pound note for every addition tae yor fam'ly ; an' though there might not be ower muckle profit in it, it wud help tae keep the pot a-boiling, says he.   But I'm thinkin' mysel',' continued my informant reflectively, 'that if Farmer New-ton were tae give up shootin' an huntin' sae muckle, an' took a turn at farmin', he'd have a less reason for complaining.'

And so we passed the time away, he regaling me with all the domestic gossip of the countryside, I interrupting him now and again to point out the historical objects of interest on either hand of us ; for, like all true countrymen, though he knew every stick and stone by the wayside, he was entirely ignorant of the past history of his vale.

We were now close on the village where my driver ended his stage, and it suddenly occurred to me to inquire, as I thanked him

---

* The author understands that this is the case in regard to some of the livings in the gift of Greenwich Hospital.

for his kindness to myself, if he knew anything of my friend's protégé at the Fair
Green Haugh.

'Well,' he replied slowly, 'I have heard as
hoo he has ta'en up wi' a convick or gaol-bord
o' that description. Wey, I canna tell. He'd
muckle better hae getten'd hissel' marrit; an'
sartinly we divvn't want that sort o' specie
up this wattor-side. We hevn't muckle gear
belike, but we prefer tae keep wor ain. He'll
be ain o' the lifting kind likelies, the same
as thae moss-troopin' fellers ye were crackin'
on aboot enoo whae divvn't seem ivvor tae
hae heard on the fifth commandment. Ye'll
be weel employed this holiday-time o' yors
wi' lookin' efter him, I's warn'd. But yo're
a lawyer chap,' he continued, 'an' dootless
ye'll find an excuse tae shift him wi'. Put on
yor wig, an' nae doot but it will tarrify him.'

I thanked the speaker for his advice somewhat ruefully, for his words exactly fitted my
own presentiment.

Having bade adieu to my postman friend,

and arranged for my heavier luggage to be
sent forward in the next carrier's cart that
might be going 'up the wattor,' I set out
across the hills to The Nook on Fair Green
Haugh with my knapsack on my back.

Two hours' walking brought me within
view of The Nook, and as I paused at the
top of the brae to drink in the well-beloved
aspect of the small 'bigging' that sheltered
in the green coign between Windy Law and
Blind Burn side, I noticed the figure of a
man carrying a small child in his arms.

I knew most of the inhabitants of the vale
by sight, but the aspect of the individual in
question was unknown to me. It was scarcely
likely he could be a shepherd's extra hand,
for the washing and shearing time was over,
and a tramp in the ordinary sense of the
term would have been, to quote from the
ornithologists, a 'rare and occasional visitor.'
Besides, he had not the appearance of a
tramp ; he walked with an easy boldness,
apparently playing with the child as he

strolled, for as I drew nearer I could hear
the child's voice gleefully crying, 'Again,
again ; do it again, funny man.'

As I drew nearer I looked at the stranger
with interest, and noted that he was a well-
made, active fellow, of good proportions.
His face was slightly scarred, as though from
small-pox, but not unpleasantly ; it was as if
the disease, suddenly repenting of spoiling a
bright and healthful countenance, had incontinently left him for another victim.

His eyes blue, his teeth, splendidly regular,
were clean and white as a hound's. Glancing
at the child, I discovered her to be Maggie,
the six-year-old child of Tom Hedley, the
herd at Fulhope Law, so I went straight up
to her and asked for a kiss as usual. ' No,'
said the diminutive flirt archly, holding her
head backwards ; ' no kiss for zoo. I's got
a new man noo,' and forthwith she buried
her curls in his neck. ' He's a nice funny
man,' she continued in another moment,
peeping forth from her hiding-place, ' an'

he's got nae mair hair on his heid than oor little puppy-dog at home.'

I glanced at her captor, and noting his cropped crown, jumped to a sure conclusion as to his identity. 'Why, 'tis none other,' thought I, 'than the protégé.' Possibly he read my thoughts ; at any rate, releasing one arm, he lifted his hand to a salute, smiling, meanwhile, in the most affable way in the world. I nodded 'Good afternoon,' and learning that the minister was within and waiting my arrival, turned my steps to the house.

After our first greetings were over he commenced to apologize again for the limited space at my disposal, but he was certain that when once I had got to know his 'protégé,' I should think no more about it. 'He is a beautiful character,' he concluded enthusiastically, 'one could tell that at a glance by the way in which children take to him.

'I met him outside just a moment ago,' I replied, 'and he certainly seems to have

won little Maggie's heart, but from my recol-
lection of her half a dozen " sweeties " would
explain that feat.   And after all,' I continued
judicially, 'some of the greatest ruffians that
ever lived were extremely fond of children.
There was Herod, of course, but he was the
exception that proves the rule.'

'Ah,' sighed my friend, 'that terrible
London atmosphere!   How it cankers the
human affections!   The theory of the law,
I believe, is that every man should be considered innocent till' he has been proved
guilty; but you lawyers, reversing this in
practice, hold every man guilty till he prove
his innocence.'

'How about his hair?' I inquired rather
unkindly.

'His hair?' my friend queried, with a
puzzled expression.   'Oh, I see what you
mean,' he continued almost immediately, endeavouring to shed a *soupçon* of a smile over
his seriously earnest countenance.   'But
don't notice that, please, or you may make

him reckless. For now is the critical time,'
he added solemnly, with the professional
manner of a physician making his diagnosis ;
' if he gets safely over this his cure may be
regarded as practically assured.

'The great thing is to believe in a man,
to cultivate little by little his sense of self-
respect ; by "believing men to be better than
they are," one may even, as has been so
well said, "make them better than they are."
In England we have always gone on a
wrong principle ; we worship success, worldly
success, far too much, and have scant sym-
pathy with the unfortunate. My friend
outside says that he stole a leg of mutton
for his starving daughter. The result is he
cannot now get a situation, and his daughter
has been taken from him, and is now in
a home. Well, if the man be treated with
contumely, he may very likely despair and
give up all hope of improvement. Treat
him well, on the other hand, and you may
yet turn him into a useful citizen.'

'You put a premium on wrong-doing,' said I, as I shook my head at his argument, smiling, however, at the impassioned face before me.

His high, narrow forehead with the ruffled upstanding hair betrayed the enthusiast; the broad, refined, and eager lips marked a perennial emotion within; his eyes, notwithstanding their wonderful clarity, had a far-away look in the depths of them; a spare form, thin wrists, and shrunken hands completed the presentation of the idealistic, mystical, Don Quixote type of human nature.

While I thus reflected, my friend continued to pour out fresh instances proving satisfactorily to any non-prejudiced mind the correctness of his theory.

'But what are you going to do with him?' I asked eventually, 'for after all that is the important thing. I mean, his being here with you may be very nice for him, but it doesn't teach him a trade, and you can't afford to keep him, I know, for long.'

'First of all,' eagerly began my friend, 'I propose to keep him long enough to re-instate him in his self-respect; secondly, to study his temperament and character thoroughly in order to discover what line of life he is best suited for, and then to get him some appropriate situation. That is the programme, and, I think, a quite practical and satisfactory one. There is no "pauperizing" here, you see; it is simply giving a man a fair chance. And now,' he continued briskly, 'come out and inspect the garden.'

The protégé, it appeared, had been making himself useful therein, which my friend thought was a highly encouraging sign, 'for,' said he, 'no bad man ever cared for gardening.'

The next few days I spent contentedly in absolute idleness, now strolling up the waterside, now smoking and reading peacefully in the little arbour behind the herbaceous border. I had almost forgotten the existence

of my *bête-noir;* he showed, indeed, a most
commendable readiness to efface himself as
much as possible from observation, and when
I chanced to pass him he seemed rather to
avoid me than to seek my company. 'Good-
morning,' I would say, if I happened to
come out of the house before breakfast for
a stroll, and find him chopping firewood,
'lovely weather, and looks like lasting, I
think.'

'Ay,' he would usually reply, with a hurried
touch to his cap, 'it's canny weather,' then
muttering something about being busy, would
incontinently hurry into the house. I took
this as a sign of grace, and was quite favour-
able to the mode of intercourse thus established. But my host, I could see, was pained
at my apparent lack of interest in his protégé ;
so the next day, finding Blythe engaged in
tying up the suckers of the honeysuckle to
the trellis of the arbour, I went boldly up
to him, determined to try and draw him
out.

'Well, and how do you like the country?'
I inquired. 'A pleasant change after town
life, eh?'

He gave me a quick, suspicious glance in
return, then muttering, 'Ay, dootless,' again
devoted himself to his occupation.

I tried again, but, meeting with no encouragement, became, I am bound to confess,
a little nettled, as though with an insub-
ordinate witness. The happy insouciance
I thought to have marked in him at our first
encounter had vanished, and ''Tis the knifing
variety, after all,' I murmured to myself, and
fell to scrutinizing him somewhat severely.
There was something about him that somehow seemed familiar to me. I determined to
probe, and see if he would wince.

'Possibly you don't care about the country?'
I suggested smoothly; 'towns, perhaps,
attract you more. York, for example, is a
nice town, and, by chance, say September 30
for a little business in the vicinity, eh?'

He looked me full in the face at this, a

very ugly smile curving his lips, as he replied abruptly, ' What is it you're wanting ?'

' I don't know that I want anything for myself,' said I, somewhat elated at the success of my conjecture, ' but I should like fair play for my friend inside. Pheasants are scarce hereabouts, but possibly other things might come in useful. I needn't specify,' I continued airily, ' to a gentleman of your intelligence ; 'twould be superfluous.'

For reply he made a bound at me, head down, and both fists outstretched. It was as the rush of the bull for the matador's flag, and my bound aside just saved me from his charge, though his right fist touched me on the chest and sent me staggering backward.

He turned, and came again ; this time I had more space for manœuvre, and the memory of an old fencing trick, learned in Angelo's school of arms, swift as a flashlight, lit within my brain. I leant forward as though to meet him like a boxer, then, as he rushed upon me, turned quickly side-

15

ways, fencing fashion, and slipped half a foot backward. He missed me by a hand's breadth ; a reek of tobacco touched me hotly on the cheek : another moment and I had leapt forward on a late 'time thrust,' and caught my antagonist neatly just behind the ear. I had been unable to put any strength into the blow, but it proved to be enough to upset his poise. He staggered, stooped, and then fell headlong on the path, scarce having time to break his fall with hand or arm.

He lay there for a moment or two, apparently half-dazed ; then, slowly picking himself up, leant back with folded arms against an apple-tree, and surveyed me with a sort of sulky resignation.

'Well, you've got the better o' me again,' said he ; 'you've the luck on your side, nae doot. "Bing lay your shero," I overheard him mutter to himself under his breath, which, taken in conjunction with his name, amply sufficed to confirm my conjecture of his gipsy origin. 'What is 't ye want wi' me?' he continued, in a louder voice.

'As I said before,' I replied slowly, seating myself upon a wooden bench in front of the arbour, 'I only require fair play for my friend within. A man of the world like yourself can easily deceive him, even to the half of his kingdom; and if he has a fancy to cure the leopard of his spots or whitewash the Ethiopian—or perhaps I might say the "Egyptian" rather—I would like the process to be as inexpensive as possible to him—you understand?' I queried of my opposite, smiling as I spoke; for I had the whip-hand of him undoubtedly, and to be unpleasant politely is part of the lawyer's art.

'To put the matter more clearly still,' I continued, for he had made no response to my suggestion, 'I think a week of fresh air and quiet seclusion in the country should be enough for any man of active habits after a period of enforced leisure; the hair, moreover, grows quickly in a country retreat, as Joshua's messengers found of old, and, briefly, what I would advise is a moonlight flitting.'

Pleased with the brevity of my peroration, I took my cigarette-case from my pocket, and, having selected a cigarette, carefully proceeded to light it with the utmost deliberation.

I had taken my eyes off him for the moment, partly in order to ascertain if the cigarette were properly alight, partly to perfect the illusion of *sang froid;* and dearly I paid for my rashness, for with a bound he was upon me.

I ducked ; but it was too late, and over I went backward, my enemy a-top of me, crash through the arbour on to the stone flagging within.

I was stunned, I suppose, for a minute or so, for I lay there wondering what had happened, and annoyed that a wasp, as I thought, should have stung me in the neck. In another moment I had discovered that

the smart was due to a bit of live cigarette-
ash that had chanced to drop inside my
collar in my fall, and I tried to put up a hand
to remove it. To my disgust, I found my
hands were knotted tightly together; my
legs, too, were bound, and, as I turned my
head, my eyes met those of my enemy,
sitting beside me on a low stool.

'The gadgi' (viz., 'gorgio,' or man of non-
gipsy race) 'is but a fool in his pride and self-
conceit,' said he ; ' he is but a tortoise, for all
his pushkin's (hare) gallop at the start.'

This was what I heard him saying as I
recovered consciousness, and as I knew that
gipsies always hide their origin, and refrain
from their language in the presence of the
'gorgios,' I felt certain he must be labour-
ing under great excitement, and momentarily
expected to see him out with his knife and
finish me there and then. Here he stooped,
and I thought my hour had come, but
apparently it was only to pick up my fallen
cigarette. Pinching off the blackened end,

he put it between his lips, and, lighting it at the other end, drew in deep breaths of tobacco-smoke.

'I don't wonder you enjoy it,' said I, as I watched his proceedings with an intense annoyance; 'successful theft is pleasant to a tchor (thief), I presume?'

'And who's the tchor in the end,' retorted he—'you or me? Speak, little gutterwhelp from the toon, that art paid to lie at so many bars (sovereigns) the lie. Your kind take a man's money, plead so ill that at the finish the "stande" (gaol) has him, while the big thief's left behind in court wi' a white wig on, an' a smile on his ugly moi (mouth). Who's the tchor, then?' he repeated with a leer, as he blew a cloud of smoke in the air. 'I 'low ye got me nabbed at York 'Sizes, but it wesn't yor doin', 'twas that dirty Jack Spraggon, who turned informer an' legged me that time. Why, ye pink-eyed toon's-spawn, if I'd my rights, an' things were as they aince was, I'd hang ye tae the nearest tree. Look there,' he cried, as, stirring me with his foot, he drew up his coat-sleeve and thrust a tattoed wrist over my eyes—'look there, d'ye ken what that is?'

I gazed with interest, for it was evidently an heraldic coat, excellently well punctured in his flesh.

'A lion rampant within a tressure fleury counter fleury, by Jove! debruised by a bar sinister,' I murmured aloud.

My thoughts went back at a bound to memories of the 'Gaberlunzie Man' of the ballad, the errant James V., and 'ane louit Johnnie Faa, Lord and Earl of Little Egypt,' but all I said was, 'Still, people don't boast of an illegitimate origin nowadays.'

'Illegitimate!' he cried angrily; 'I'll teach ye manners, ye ——' but here a step sounded on the path outside, and in another moment my host peered in at the doorway.

'Tut—tut—tut,' said my friend, removing his glasses from his nose in his agitation, 'dear, dear! what can have happened? Speak, Ned; explain, Will.'

My adversary rose to his feet, saluted our interrogator somewhat shamefacedly, and, pointing to myself, replied, 'He wes sae impiddent wi' me I'd just tae teach him a lesson, but nae harm's done.'

'Oh,' cried my little friend, and he positively wrung his hands in his distress, 'but you shouldn't,' and here he looked at us reproachfully in turn. Then a happy thought seemed to rise in his brain. 'We must forget all about this unhappy occurrence,' cried he; 'we will not inquire into it, but will shake hands all round, and begin afresh.'

So saying he immediately knelt down, undid my bandages, and helped me to rise from the floor. 'Now,' he cried, and seized hold of our respective hands.

'Well,' said my antagonist, 'I bear no malice, but keep yor tongue a bit civiler i' future.'

'And refrain from pheasants and legs of mutton,' I nearly retorted, but stayed my tongue in time, and the three of us shook hands promptly all round, as desired. I was willing enough to shake hands because I felt I had been in error in taunting my antagonist, but I was not prepared for the reproof my host had in store for me, as he put his arm through mine, and led me away for a stroll up the brae.

'Oh, how could you do it?' he said. 'You must have stung him beyond endurance, and you promised, you remember, to respect him.'

'I only told him the truth,' I replied sulkily. 'As a matter of fact, I recognised in him the first individual I ever had the pleasure of getting convicted—at York Assizes — pheasant - poaching, stoning a keeper, etc. One's first conviction is like one's first love—one can't forget it.'

'Ah, but if it is so, that is just an incident in that past career of his which is quite dead and buried now; you see yourself how annoyed he was at your bringing it up against him. Of course, his conduct was inexcusable,' he hastily added, suddenly remembering doubtless that he was my host, ' but this vigour of resentment proves to my mind the genuineness of his repentance.'

It was hopeless to argue, so I turned the subject, inwardly resolving that I would leave on the morrow.

After supper that evening I went outside to smoke, and there lingered long, enjoying the soft, luminous northern twilight.

The murmur of the stream in the valley trembled amidst the silence of the night, as of some old monk telling his beads in the solitude of a vast cathedral. Suddenly a discordant singing sounded down the vale. 'Some roysterer,' thought I with disgust. 'I suppose there must have been a wedding or some festivity of that sort.'

The sounds rose and fell fitfully, but grew gradually louder. It was evident someone

was coming 'up the wattor,' and I waited to
see who the disturber of our quiet could be.

The last corner had apparently been
turned, for now I could hear the voice
distinctly. 'The protégé again, by Jove!'
I groaned.

I meditated instant flight, but a fit of
laughter caught me, and I stayed. Out of
the gray twilight a toper lurched up to the
gate on which I leant, and, steadying himself,
momentarily peered into my face.

'No malish, little Wool-shack, eh?' quoth
he with a grin. Then, becoming confidential,
he leant forward and whispered, 'Drink ye
for a "bar," turn an' turn about,' producing
as he spoke a most suspicious-looking black
bottle.

'Look here,' said I, 'why did you come to
this place?'

'It's a free-sh country,' replied my opposite
solemnly, 'an' wanderin's my trade, an' the
wee big bairn upstairs, he's ta'en a sort o'
woman's fancy for us. Noo, Wull Blythe's

like his ancient forbears, royal Wull Faa, an the lave, an' he cannot say nae to a woman, though he'll ne'er tak' a look frae a man.'

'Well, good-night,' I said, 'and don't wake the big bairn upstairs.'

It was some time before I finished packing, and after that was done I sat down and had another pipe by the window. I was just dozing off when a smell of burning seemed to creep in upon my nostrils, and the atmosphere grew thicker to my sub-consciousness.

'It can't be anything,' I murmured inwardly, and tried to recede still further into the dark grove of sleep, but a step outside my door effectually roused me.

A light gleamed upon me. 'Come, my friend, come quick; I fear the house is on fire,' cried my host at the doorway; 'throw on a coat, wet your blankets, and follow me upstairs at once with them.'

I rushed upstairs headlong some few seconds after, and stumbled over a prostrate form on the small garret landing, a reek of

whisky giving me assurance of its identity.
I rose hastily, and passed into the room
beyond, where, amidst heavy smoke-wreaths,
I perceived my host, now beating burning
bedding with his hands, and again stamping
with his feet upon smouldering coverings on
the floor.

I did my best to help him, and we
succeeded shortly in getting the better of the
conflagration. After emptying buckets of
water over bed and bedding, we waited for
some minutes to ascertain if any hidden fire
lingered anywhere.

'I think it will be all right now,' said my
host; 'but come, we must look after my
poor friend outside — I fear he is badly
burned. Poor fellow, he was lying in bed
stupefied with the smoke. I suppose he
must have fallen asleep reading, and the
candle must have set fire somehow to the
bed-clothes or curtain.'

He had scarcely finished speaking when
he swayed suddenly, and before I could reach

out an arm, had fallen to the ground in a dead faint. I lifted him up and carried him downstairs at once, and found that he was rather severely burnt about the hands.

After I had restored him to consciousness as best I could and dressed his hurts, I proceeded, at my friend's earnest entreaty, to look after the protégé, who was still lying prostrate on the garret landing, absolutely unconscious and hopelessly intoxicated.

He was badly burnt on one arm, and scorched down one side of his body. Appearances seemed to show that he must have thrown off the counterpane and blankets on to the floor, that there they must have become ignited either from his fallen pipe or candle, and eventually have set fire to one side of the bed.

The doctor had to be sent for, and for a week the protégé was kept in bed ; when he did come down again he was as contrite as possible, and I carefully avoided all mention of the disaster, for I had a dim feeling of guilt in the matter, suspecting that he went down the valley that evening to the alehouse in consequence of his excitement at his triumph over myself.

Now that he was about again, and my friend too was quite restored, I determined to depart, and the next morning went down early to the Frolic to enjoy a last bathe.

I was sitting on a shelf of rock above a deep pool, drying myself slowly after my swim, when I heard sounds below me. Looking out from my shelter, I saw Blythe, who appeared to be about to follow my example. His procedure, however, was curious; for first he cast his cap upon the waters, then carefully deposited what looked to me like a Bible on his coat on the bank, and, finally, having looked about him stealthily, took off his shoes and proceeded to ford the burn.

' He's off,' I thought to myself, then cried to him, ' Holloa ! what's up ?'

He stood stock-still in mid-stream like one

petrified, then, perceiving me, waded slowly
to shore.

'Noo, don't ye blab tae Mistor Rutherford,'
he said, as he came close up underneath
where I was standing. 'I's awa aff. I
cannot stay, but I doot the little man will
be sair troubled aboot it, sae let him think
on as that I'm drooned, wi' the Bible there
tae show I's a convarted character, for he's
been one tae many for Blythe, an' I wud'na
like him tae grieve ower my disappointing
him. I cam' for a bit fun, but it's turning
tae seriousness noo, an' I can't bide any mair,
that's a sartinty.'

I don't know whether I acted wrongly or
not, but I fell in with his view of the situation,
and when I had finished my dressing he had
already stolen out of sight.

I stayed on another week after this, and
during that time successfully concealed my
connivance at the protégé's flight.

The discovery of his cap and coat was
considered proof of his having been drowned,

and the Bible, borrowed from himself for the occasion, provided at once a consolation for my friend and a rebuke to my scepticism.

I spent a night in Oldcastle on my way back to town, and chance took me through one of the most thickly populated, though not most aristocratic, quarters of the city. It was a fine night, and I had prolonged my stroll unconsciously. Suddenly the swing-door of a public-house was thrown back violently, and a man came hurtling through, and fell with a thud on the pavement beside me; a face peered through the aperture of the doors for a moment, and in a flash I recognised it.

The gentleman who had been thus igno-miniously 'chucked out' slowly pulled him-self together, collected his faculties and his hat with difficulty, uttered some violent and abusive epithets, then slowly staggered off down the street with drunken dignity.

I went inside the aforesaid doors. My eyes had not deceived me, for there was the

16

protégé behind the counter in his new capacity
of barman and 'chucker out.'   He signed to
me to follow him into the 'snug,' and there
confided to me that he had got a permanent
job for the first time in his life.

'Here,' said he, 'is a bar' (sovereign);
'send it along tae Mister Rutherford, an'
tell him I's alive an' hearty, an' that I canna
rest till I's paid for the blankets an' beddin'
I burnt the other week.   Mind,' says he,
'ye're not tae say where I am, but tell him
I've a situation, an's givin' satisfaction.'

'Well,' thought I to myself, as I returned
to my hotel, 'if my friend hasn't reformed
the protégé, he has come at all events as
near to success as is good for the ordinary
mortal.'

THE SPANISH DOUBLOON

RANSACKING Jake's treasury one afternoon, I made an unexpected find —no less than a Spanish doubloon hidden away in an old sporran of a great-uncle of his.

The history of the fox-marked rapier, of the blood-stained tress of hair found at Cawnpore, and of the yellow robe of the Brahmin, I knew already; but the heavy Spanish coin suggested something of a different order.

'Come,' said I, holding it up so as to attract his attention, 'tell me the tale connected with this—something to do with a pirate, or the Spanish Main, I dare swear.'

Jake smiled quaintly as he fingered the coin with deliberation. 'Weel, it's a queer

16—2

tale, sartinly, that's connected wi' yon coin, but all I can tell ye is what my aunt telled me langsyne, when she presented it to me on my joining the sarvice, just before I left for India.

'Noo, my aunt, ye mun ken, was a widow woman who lived on a bit property she had left her doon at the small, ootlandish-named seaport, as it was then, o' Bocca Chica, on the Northumberland coast.

'There was a man there she kenned nicely —in fact, she aye said afterwards, wi' a shudder at the thocht o't, that at one time he wanted to marry wi' her—who cut a big figure i' the place, by name Isaac Stephenson—"Black Isaac," as he was mair usually styled. It seems he had been bred and born i' the place, but had run awa to sea i' his youth, an' after many voyagings here an' there turns up again wi' pockets fu' o' siller, and a wee, misbegotten heathen dwarf o' a Malay as his attendant.

'The dwarf called hissel' Chilpo, or some

such uncanny name, an' was a kind o' body-servant an' clerk an' dirty-job man to Isaac. But Isaac never let on where he picked him up, an' Chilpo was a sour-tempered little deil, whom maist folks were terrified o'; sae nae-body e'er kenned muckle o' his antecedents or ancestry.

'Weel, Isaac, on his settling doon again at home, set up i' business as a shipowner an' broker, an' carried on a large business as an exporter o' coals, an' did a bit, as maist everybody did i' those days, i' the smuggling line—salt, an' lace, an' brandy, ye ken. He had siller, as I said, when he started his new trade, though naebody kenned hoo he had come by it; but it was no lang before he was the richest man i' the toon, an' folk began to talk weel o' him, an' praise him up as a good citizen as was a credit to the toon, an' ask him to open bazaars for them, an' suchlike.

'There was just one strange thing aboot him, an' that was that the womenfolk couldn't abide him. E'en after he had made hisself

the richest man i' the toon, he could ne'er
get hissel' married, though 'twas said my
aunt, when he took up wi' religion, had aince
had a thocht o' him, but no for lang, for there
was suthin' aboot him that tarrified her when
it came near the point.

'He was no ill-favoured neither, for I
mind seein' him mysel' as a lad aince I was
stayin' wi' my aunt—a tall, poo'erfu', black-
haired man, wi' heavy eyebrows, an' a lustfu'
sort o' eye—half hectorin', half cowardly.
But he had a cruel sort o' look aboot him—
thick-lipped, an' greedy, sweaty sort o' hands.

'Weel, after a good few years o' prosperity
he turned sort o' sickly-like, an' for the first
time i' his life began to think upon his latter
end, an' at the finish takes up wi' a sect o'
Bible Christians, or Christadelphians, or some
such body, who were glad to get hold o'
such a rich, influential sort o' person withoot
askin' ower mony questions.

'Weel, he gans to his chapel, an' he
prays, an' he gies his testimony, an' calls

hissel' all sorts o' names, but was ay cautious no to gie ower mony details o' his sins, an' the good folk were highly edified by it, my aunt amangst them, an' asked him for subscriptions for every sort o' charity.

'But Chilpo, he couldna stand this sudden right-about-face, for there was nae releegion at aal i' his wee, misshapen anatomy, naething but love o' siller, and beastly, secretive pleasures o' opium drams an' such like. An' he mutinies against it, an' cusses an' swears to hissel' i' his pigeon-English talk, for Isaac by degrees began to hae his doots aboot the lawfu'ness o' smugglin' an' saeforth, an' Chilpo's wages an 'profits dootless wud suffer by his maister's scruples.

'Consequence was, there grew to be bad blood betwixt maister an' man, an' folk could hear them quarrelling inside the office o' nights, till at the finish there's a grand flare-up, Isaac seemingly strikin' Chilpo, an' Chilpo clickin' his maister wi' his knife.

'Chilpo gets the bag for that, Isaac no

daurin' to prosecute him, for he kenned ower
muckle.   But he disna leave the toon ; just
hangs aboot, doggin' Isaac's footsteps, an'
cussin' to hissel' i' his queer, ootlandish way
o' talk.   "Him coward," he would mutter,
"but Chilpo brave man.   He no take no
blowee.   Chilpo hang Isaac—hang himselfee
—no matter—Chilpo fear nozzin'," an' he
would gnash wi' his white teeth savagely
like a mad dog as he saw Isaac pass along
the street.

'His heart was just as black as his sweaty,
black phiznommy, an' he properly haunted
Isaac till he fair plagued him to death.

'One Sabbath, when there was a great
function on at Isaac's chapel, he actually
follows him in, an' sat sneerin' an' mimickin'
an' makin' game o' Isaac as he prayed an'
groaned, an' confessed to bein' a muckle
great sinner i' the past, till Isaac was near
mad wi' rage an' terror.   He tried to pray,
but the words wouldn't come richt, an' the
sweat poured aff his brow, they said, till folk

thought he was about to hae a fit or seizure o' some sort.

'At the finish he gies it up, an', staggerin' on to his feet, points i' a frenzied sort o' way to Chilpo sittin' there below him, an' cries oot loud : " It's the deil, it's the deil ! Drive him awa ; drive him oot o' the holy place ! I tell ye he's sin hissel'. See the sooty face on him !"

' " Ugh ! Black Isaac, him coward !" shouts Chilpo, standin' up on his seat. " Him sky-pilot nowee, no goodee any more. Once a timee diffelent ; good pilate once, grand pilate with Chilpo ; men's pilate, women's pilates, temple's pilates, all sorts pilates. Oh yez ; huzza ! Dam good timee then ; ping-pang, click-click, plenty moneys, plenty grogs, plenty funee. O yez ; Chilpo, he knowee." The little heathen chuckled to himself, makin' uncanny motions wi' his hands o' throat-cuttin' an' liquor-drinkin' an' fillin' his pockets wi' siller.

' " Him hipple - clite nowee," continued

Chilpo, shoutin' aloud to all the chapel-folks who hadn't recovered theirsels from their amazement; "dam hipple-clite! Why, him worship the debbil like Chilpo former timee. Him no use for prayee; him dam-ee, curs-ee; him Church's pilate, women's pilate, then burnee together. Oh yes, him lemember allight; askee him," an' wi' that he points his finger at Isaac, whose face was workin' in a frightful fashion, his eyes starin' this way an' that, wi' no meanin' i' them, his lips black, an' his mouth slobberin'; then sudden he starts to run, but catches his foot an' falls full length doon on the floor an' drums wi' his hands amangst the cushions.

'There was a panic at that; half o' the women faints dead awa, the bairns scream, and some o' the men drives Chilpo, still chucklin' to himself, oot at the door wi' blows, whilst others attend to Isaac lyin' wi' his head covered i' the dusty cushions an' his hands hard a-grip o' the seat-stanchions.

'They loosens his grasp wi' difficulty, but

lifts him up at the finish wi' a shockin' face on him, an' a senseless tongue that babbled aboot a parrot. Some said it mun ha' been i' reference someway to some wicked episode i' his past life which Chilpo kenned o' an' alluded to i' the chapel. Maybe a parrot had been left the sole survivor after a sack, ye ken, an Isaac couldna forget the scene. Anyways, Chilpo, the dam cunnin' little de'il, kenned o' the hidden sore i' Isaac's mind, an' laid a cruel finger on 't wi' the blackest malice. An' there was nae doot aboot the outcome o't, for Isaac was gone clean daft, an' died not long afterwards i' the asylum.

'Weel, they gied him a big buryin', for his brethren i' the chapel said they believed he was a true repentant sinner, an' forbye that he had left a good bit siller amangst them, which would dootless assist them to that conclusion; an' as there had been some body-snatchin' lately, they determined to form a small watch committee to keep guard at the graveside for a night or two.

'Weel, the watch was composed o' some decent elderly folk, who didn't trash theirselves ower the job ; an' mevvies the funeral festivities had delayed them a bit, for they didn't arrive at the graveyard till aboot half-past ten o' the clock.

'It was ane o' thae tempestuous October nights, wi' half a gale blowin', an' clouds gallopin', wi' flittin's o' moonlight like jockeys ridin' 'em ; an' when they came nigh to the graveside, an' saw a dark, misshapen sort o' a figure plyin' an axe vigorously, an' heard a thud, thud, same as ye may when passin' by a butcher's shop any day, why, they turned tail and fled, the most o' them stumblin' this way an' that amangst the headstones.

'Two o' them, though, was a bit bolder, an' pressed on up to the graveside, whereupon the little black demon figure thuds doon his axe wi' a sickenin' sound, then dives awa into the darkness, screechin' oot : '' Chilpo, Chilpo! he makee sicker, he makee sicker !" and therewith vanished frae Bocca Chica.

'As for the doubloon,' concluded Jake, spinning it into the air as he spoke, 'it was found amangst some leavin's o' Chilpo's at his lodgin's, an' sold wi' some other trinkets to pay some small debts he had left behind him.

'My aunt bought it up as a memento o' the marcifu' preservation she had had frae marryin' wi' a buccaneer; an' when I said good-bye to her on startin' for India, she presented it to me, wi' an admonition ne'er to have any traffic wi' dwarfs or pirates.'

THE END

www.ingramcontent.com/pod-product-compliance
Lightning Source LLC
Chambersburg PA
CBHW031418020726
47499CB00005B/1490